HOUSE of the STAR

*For Jenny—
who knows all about
white Horses between
the worlds—
gh

Solstice
2010*

HOUSE
of the
STAR

CAITLIN BRENNAN

STARSCAPE

A TOM DOHERTY ASSOCIATES BOOK
NEW YORK

This is a work of fiction. All of the characters, organizations, and events portrayed in this novel are either products of the author's imagination or are used fictitiously.

HOUSE OF THE STAR

Copyright © 2010 by Caitlin Brennan

A Starscape Book
Published by Tom Doherty Associates, LLC
175 Fifth Avenue
New York, NY 10010

www.tor-forge.com

ISBN 978-0-7653-2037-7

First Edition: November 2010

Printed in October 2010 in the United States of America by RR Donnelley, Harrisonburg, Virginia

0 9 8 7 6 5 4 3 2 1

To all the Large White Objects on the farm,
especially Pandora, who loves to be a Star

HOUSE
of the
STAR

CHAPTER I

Between the lake of fire and the river of ice, Elen faced the truth. She was lost. The road that had been so wide and straight when she began had dwindled into the faint line of a footpath. Now even that was gone. Her stolen map showed neither the world ahead nor the world behind. Whenever she tried to turn back, the baying of hounds sent her stumbling forward again.

As the road melted away to nothing in front of her, the hounds' cries faded away. She stood on the barren hillside, exhausted and footsore and weak with hunger and thirst. Long hours ago when there was still a road to follow, she had stumbled as she ran, and a bone-white hound had sprung upon her. Its snapping jaws had torn the pack of provisions from her back and the talisman from around her neck, the worn silver medallion that should have guided and protected her.

She pressed her hands to her eyes. The ice had frozen the tears, and the fire had burned them away. She kept seeing things on the edge of vision, skeletal horses and ghostly riders, watching, hovering, making no sound. Sometimes, if she slanted her glance just so, she saw the one who led them: a tall shape with a crown of spreading antlers. His eyes on her were dark and still.

Above her, winged things circled, waiting for her to fall. Those, she saw clearly. They looked as small as songbirds, but one had come down when she first stumbled onto the hill, and its wings had shadowed the whole of the summit.

It tilted its scaly head and fixed her with a cold yellow eye, and clashed its long hooked beak. She tensed to run, as if anything could escape that monstrous thing, but it turned and beat upward in a swirl of leathery wings.

Its stench nearly felled her—and it told her why the creature waited. It fed on dead things. She was alive.

It would wait, its eye had said.

She was not going to die. She clung to that. She was going to live.

In her head she held a picture of a barn, a pasture,

a herd of horses. It was green and quiet, peaceful—safe. She only had to find it.

"You *will* go," the queen had said to Elen a day or an eon ago, far away in Ymbria.

Her gown was the color of the night sky, scattered with gems like stars, and her crown was set with a white stone like the moon. She was tall and dark and terrible, and her will was as strong as cold iron.

Elen was dusty and muddy and covered with a spring mantle of horsehair; her thick black hair was snarled half out of its braid. The queen's summons had brought her up from the stables with no time to stop or bathe or make herself presentable.

She faced the royal majesty with great respect and perfectly equal stubbornness. "I can't."

"This is not a matter of can or will," said the queen. "This is *must*."

Elen shook her head. "No. I won't go."

The queen took off her crown and laid it on a table. Its weight had marked her forehead deeply, but when she rubbed it, Elen could see that the ache came from deeper inside. "Why, daughter? This has been your dream since you were old enough to clamber up on a pony. Now you can have it. You can travel to Earth, live in the House of the Star, spend your days with and care for and even, gods willing, ride the only creatures that can travel safely along the worldroads. Isn't that what you've always wanted?"

"I want to be a worldrider," Elen said. "I want it with all my heart. But if I do what you are trying to make me do, that's not what I'll get. You're trying to pretend it's about the horses, but it's not. It's about the same war that has torn us apart for thousands of years, and it will be just as useless as all the other attempts to make it stop. I'm to go to Earth, meet the king's son from Caledon, and let myself be forced to marry him. The worldrunners are just a bribe to get me there."

The queen sank down into the chair beside the table. The silk of her gown rustled; the jewels and the pearls rattled against the carved wood of the chair. "No one will force you to marry anyone," she said. "This invitation comes from Earth. You only need to go, join a group of young people in the House of the Star, ride and care for their horses, live on Earth for a season, and see what comes of it. That's all. How is that so difficult?"

Elen shook her head so hard her braid gave way altogether and sent her hair tumbling down over her back and shoulders. "Don't you understand? It *can't* be that simple. Friendship, Earth said. Mutual understanding. Liking, if possible, between royal offspring of the two most relentless enemies in all the worlds. Doesn't that sound lovely? Doesn't it sound too easy for words?"

"It doesn't sound easy at all," the queen said. "It sounds like a challenge worthy of the greatest of our heroes: to meet a Caledonian face to face, and learn to forget our whole long history of hatred, and make a friend. Horses are the key, says the Master of the Star. Earth is neutral ground, and the horses from whose stock the worldrunners come are creatures of such power and wonder in their own right that even he can't tell us what they may decide to do. But he is willing to trust them. And so, perforce, are we."

Horses of any kind, let alone worldrunners, were a great lure and attraction, and Elen wanted them desperately. But this was too cruel a lie for her to bear. She cried out against it. "But that's not true! There's got to be something else they're not saying. Some thing they want, that we'll find out if I get there. Some plan they're keeping secret. You know what it has to be. They want Ymbria and Caledon bound together—and how does that ever get done? By royal marriage. I'd rather not have the horses at all than have them for a few days and then see them taken away, either because I've been hauled off into Caledon, or because I refuse and have been sent back home, and the worldroads have been closed forever to anyone from Ymbria."

"Caledon, too," the queen said, "if it comes to that. Which I hope it will not. But, Elen, you must understand. This is the last chance. The other worlds along the roads have had enough of our fighting that spills over onto them and does them such terrible damage. Faerie itself has lost patience. The Horned King and his deadly Hunt would have closed us off well before this if Earth had not spoken for us. We need what the roads bring us: trade and knowledge and the arts and magic and medicines that heal our sick and nourish our land and make our crops grow richer and stronger to feed our people. Without those things, we wither and die."

"I know that!" Elen said. "I just can't do this. I *can't.* I'm not the kind of person you need. Why don't you send Margali? All she cares about is boys and dresses and more boys. *She* would be perfectly happy to attach herself to a royal Caledonian, as long as he has a pretty face and a large fortune."

"Elen!" the queen said. Her tone was like a slap. "Horses make your sister ill, and horses are a requirement. You love them more than anyone else in this family. I had thought you loved Ymbria, too."

Those were terrible words. Elen flinched.

"You leave in the morning," her mother said. "Be ready to ride."

Elen was dismissed. She opened her mouth to refuse, but what could she say that she had not already said?

People were clamoring at the door. The royal council was meeting—again. Messengers were lined up six deep, each with an urgent dispatch that the queen must answer immediately. Elen was keeping them all from getting their work done.

"Lying, treacherous, murdering monsters," she muttered as she trudged back to the stables. "Never trust a Caledonian. Never give him your horse or your hound or, by all you hold holy, your daughter. No one knows that better than Mother. Why does she even try?"

Elen brought out her favorite mount, the spotted pony, whose name was Brychan. He was fresh and eager and delighted to see his saddle, though the day was getting on and the sky was spitting sleet. No one was there to stop her: the stablehands were all at dinner, having fed the horses and tucked them in for the night.

She meant to set her mind in order while she rode, and somehow bring herself to face what she had to do. Her mother would be terribly disappointed. That hurt. But the more she thought about doing this thing, even for Ymbria, even for her mother, the less she could stand it.

There were others who could go, who could tolerate both horses and, within limits, Caledon; who would not be devastated when the real plan came out and the promise of worldrunners proved to be a lie. Elen did not see how it could be true. Nothing that Caledon agreed to could ever be anything but treacherous.

"There's no good reason it has to be me, and every reason it shouldn't be," Elen said to the pony's ears.

They flicked in response; he tossed his shaggy mane and bucked lightly. She loosened rein and let him go.

The wind cut sharp and keen. The sleet stung her cheeks. The ground was solid underfoot—which was not always true in these days of endless war and renegade magics. The storm was perfectly mortal and ordinary, and because of that, it was wonderful.

The pony bucked and plunged across the field, then straightened into a steady canter. She aimed him toward the band of trees that edged the far pasture.

It was quiet out here. All the rush and bustle and uproar of the royal house was behind her, calming down a little with the approach of evening, but it would never be completely calm. The woods were dark already, silent but for the rattle of sleet and the soft hiss of wind in the icy branches.

Brychan halted so suddenly that Elen nearly pitched over his head. His ears nearly touched at the tips, quivering with alertness. He blew out a ferocious snort.

Out of the shadows of the wood, down a track that had never been straight before and might never be straight again, a great white horse came striding. All the light that was left in the world gathered in that long arched nose and that tall, solid body and those deep wise eyes. They looked into Elen's for a moment that stretched into forever, and for that moment she saw herself on the wide white back, wearing a broad-brimmed hat and a long dark coat and tall black boots.

That was a worldrunner. It was a mare, Elen saw as she cantered past, as light on those big round feet as a much smaller horse. Her rider, who was dressed just as Elen had been in the dream or vision or heartfelt wish, took no notice of the girl on the pony. But the grey mare did. She noticed, and she remembered.

Tears streamed down Elen's face, freezing in the wind. In all the years she had seen worldrunners come and go, none of them had ever looked straight at her and recognized her, and said to the deepest part of her heart, *You. I know you. I know everything about you, everything you are or ever wanted to be.*

She wanted this more than anything. She wanted it so much, it made her heart pound and her throat lock and her eyes go dark. But now she realized what she wanted, and it was so much more, so much deeper and stronger than she had ever dreamed, that she could hardly breathe.

It was too much. Elen who was afraid of nothing, who could leave the boldest of her brothers crying in the dirt while she dared to climb the highest tree or ride the wildest horse, was terrified. If she was right and her mother was wrong, and Earth's offer was a lie and she would have her chance at worldrunners for a little while only to lose it all for Ymbria's sake, that would be grievous. But if she got it—if after all she could get and keep this enormous, amazing, wonderful, profoundly frightening thing, could she even begin to be good enough for it?

Elen the brave, Elen the obstinate, Elen the royal princess of Ymbria, turned her spotted pony on his haunches and fled from the thing she wanted most in any world.

Elen rode Brychan back to the stables in a blur of wind and sleet and almost-panic. The part of her that was a horse girl knew enough not to run the pony off his feet, so that by the time he reached the barn and the sleet turned to snow, he had cooled down.

She was calmer now, the kind of calm that lies at the heart of a storm. All the fears and doubts and horrors still swirled around her, but she took care of Brychan as if none of them existed. She rubbed him as dry as she could, covered him with a blanket and fed him a hot mash and left him in peace.

Her own dinner was waiting. She was not hungry at all. She could not face her mother or the rest of her family or, worst of all, the worldrider. Not tonight.

She had a plan now. She knew what she had to do. It did not matter if what she did was reasonable or sensible or even sane. She had to do it. That was all.

She made a show of shutting herself in her room and calling for a tray from the kitchen. When it came, she ate everything on it, no matter how her stomach rebelled.

Her mind was made up. She would go—but not to Earth. Once she was out of the way, someone else could be chosen to do this great and terrible thing. Someone better; more willing. Someone who really was strong enough.

Elen would find sanctuary far down the worldroad, with horses and pasture and a stable where she could earn her keep. The worlds were full of such places. Every world had horses or some kind of animal like them, though only Earth had worldrunners. Worldrunners could be born nowhere else; no one who had tried to change that had ever succeeded.

As for how she would get away from Ymbria without a worldrunner, that was the difficult part; but Elen's head was full of stories. In some of them, especially the oldest ones, a person with a firm will and a clear image in her mind could make the worldroads lead her where she wanted to go. It helped if she had something to focus on, a jewel or a map or a talisman. But she could do it.

Elen had the will. She could find a map of the worldroads. She knew where there was a talisman, though it was old and worn and had no magic left in it. She even had a destination. It was a world called

Hesperia, where the sweetest apples came from, and a cordial that could heal the heart's ills. She had met a girl from there once, a horse girl like her, who had been traveling with her father to trade apples for the sweet spices and the fine horses of Ymbria.

Irena might have forgotten Elen long ago, but Elen had always remembered the place Irena had described, to which the three geldings and the one bay mare were to go. It was a place of wide rolling meadows and little streams, and grass as rich as any in the worlds.

Surely they would need a stablehand there, or even a trainer. Or somewhere nearby would welcome such a person. Anywhere that had horses, really, except Earth itself, would do.

Macsen the librarian was asleep in the palace library, face down in a book, snoring. An army could have invaded and he would barely have stirred.

There was no one else among the shelves and tables and chests of books so old that some of them had been written before worldrunners came to Ymbria. The book of maps that Elen needed was on a shelf up near the high ceiling; it needed a ladder and a far stretch that nearly sent her tumbling to the floor, but she recovered it and herself with no bones broken. With the book lying heavy and solid in the pocket of her coat, she trod softly toward the far end of the room.

Tall glass cases gleamed in the dimness. They were full of interesting oddments, lesser treasures and bits of history that were not so precious that they needed to be hidden away in the royal treasury. Among the tarnished trophies and the coins of ancient realms hung a medallion on a faded ribbon. It looked like a silver coin rubbed smooth with age. On one side was the image of a nine-spoked wheel. Elen had never seen the other: it was hidden against the back of the case.

Her breath came hard as if she had been running a race. The lock on the case was sealed with a spell, but the steel of Elen's lock-pick broke it with a pop and a spark. The pick, which had begun life as a hairpin, leaped out of Elen's fingers. She hissed in startlement and shook them hard: they throbbed and stung.

Gingerly she retrieved the hairpin. It was harmless again, and so was the lock.

Some skills that Elen's more interesting friends had taught her were more useful than others, though her mother might not agree about this one. She opened the case as quietly as she could, darting glances at Macsen, who had not moved a muscle in all that time.

The contents of the case had no such spell on them as had warded the lock. The medallion felt like ordinary silver, cool and smooth; its back was covered with writing too faded and worn to read. Legend said that such baubles had held enormous power once. If that was true, this one had lost the last of it long ago.

Still, along with the book of maps, it was the best chance Elen had to fulfill her plan, short of stealing a worldrunner—and she was not quite crazy enough to do that. She hung the talisman around her neck, tucking it into her shirt. It was cold against her skin, but it warmed slowly as she made her soft-footed way past Macsen and out of the library.

The cooks were so busy with dinner that they barely noticed the bits of bread and meat and fruit and cheese that Elen plucked from passing bowls and platters. The hardest part was taking it all and packing it in a knapsack and walking away from the only home she had ever known.

She had to do it. She kept telling herself that.

She went on foot. Brychan would have carried her; he was brave and he loved her. But she could not do it to him. He was no worldrunner; he was not born and bred to travel the worldroads.

She went out alone into the storm. Her mind was set on the road she needed to find and the place where she wanted to go. The medallion proved useful after all: it helped to serve as a focus. She could see her starting point as the wheel's hub, and the track she needed as one of the spokes. She was careful not to let her vision waver, and not to get distracted.

She could have taken one of the roads that ran straight out from the palace itself, but that was too public, even at night and in a snowstorm. Instead she went back to the place where she had first seen the white mare.

The worldroad was still there, as if it waited for the mare to come back to it. If Elen had been paying close enough attention, she would have been suspicious, but it took most of her strength of will to keep her mind fixed on what she needed to do and where she needed to go.

Worldroads were things of Faerie, of wild and untamed magic, and like all wild magic, they were full of snares and deceptions. Elen was too busy keeping her wish in her mind to notice much else. She only had to stay on the straight track, she told herself, and take care to know, all the way down to the bone, where she wanted to go.

Worlds like pearls strung on a string, oases of order and safety and, mostly, peace, surrounded by the wildness that was Faerie. Far down the string from Ymbria, and far away from either Earth or Caledon, a world called Hesperia. Far, fair, and green. And horses. Above all, horses.

Instead, the road gave her ice and fire and a pack of

harrying hounds, and cast her on a hillside in Faerie, in the most dangerous and treacherous of all realms that were.

She would die here. Her soul would wander the borderlands of Faerie forever, lost and forgotten. She would never see her mother or her people or her world again.

After a moment or an hour or an age, hooves clattered on stone. Elen lowered her hands from her eyes, blinking. The light of this place was dazzling bright and yet had no source: no sun or moon or star.

The shape that loomed over her was as white as the sky. It lowered its long head and warmed her with its sweet-scented breath. She was safe now, it said without words: a feeling so deep it sank all the way to the bottom of her. She wrapped her arms around the grey mare's neck and clung for her life's sake.

The mare was alone. She wore no saddle or bridle and carried no rider. Still, there was no mistaking that tall and massive body or that strong arched profile with its dark, wise eye.

Elen looked into that eye and found the mare's name there. It came to Elen first as a feeling: a sense of snow and clouds and peaceful whiteness. The word that described that feeling was an Earth word, and it was a name: *Blanca*.

"Blanca," Elen said. Her voice was as raw as her throat. "Please. Take me—"

The rest would not come as words. She held the image of the horses and the pasture and the world called Hesperia inside her head, and hoped that Blanca could see it, too.

Blanca knelt. *Mount,* that meant.

Elen took a breath to steady her hammering heart. The confusion of doubt and fear that had driven her away from the mare and from Ymbria was still there, but the terror of Faerie was stronger. She wound her fingers in Blanca's mane and swung her leg over the broad white back. When she was secure, the mare surged upright.

Elen was in Blanca's power now. All she could do was hold on and hope.

When Blanca strode out, there was a road under her feet, straight and clear through the wilds of Faerie. Elen dared not loose her death grip on Blanca's mane to hunt in her pocket for the book of maps. Blanca was a worldrunner; she must know where to go.

Elen held fast to her vision of Hesperia. Blanca moved from a walk into a long-strided, smooth but powerful canter. The hills of Faerie rolled past, soft and green at first, but growing sharper and more jagged as the road ran on. The light never changed; time passed, it must, but there was no way to judge how fast or how slow it was passing.

With a worldrunner under her, Elen had nothing to fear. No hounds stalked her. No skeletal Hunt haunted the road behind her.

Blanca's calm washed over Elen. The mare knew where she was going, and she fully expected to get there, safe and whole and with her rider still on her back.

Elen had always been able to feel what horses were feeling, and mostly she could guess what they were thinking. They did most of their talking with their bodies, with the slant of an ear or the turn of a head or the wrinkle of a nostril.

This was like that, but it was stronger than anything Elen had felt before. What had scared her in Ymbria, and what still made it hard to get enough air into her lungs, was how *right* it felt. This big white creature belonged here, striding along under her, taking her where she needed to go. One moment, Elen had been her sturdy and independent self, riding any horse she could get a leg over, loving a few and liking most of them. The next, she had found herself so much a part of Blanca that she could hardly tell where she left off and the mare began.

Blanca seemed perfectly comfortable with that. Elen had never been raised or taught to expect it. None of the stories talked of any such thing. Worldriders were riders and messengers, trained to navigate the worldroads on the backs of worldrunners. Worldrunners were a particular strain of horses from Earth, who had to be born there and could not be born or bred elsewhere. People had tried it over and over; the best they could hope for was that the mares never got in foal at all. If they did, the foals died, or were born so twisted and broken that they could not survive.

Elen squeezed her eyes shut. This was doing her no good at all. She had to stop panicking over the horse and remember where she was going. *Hesperia. Pastures. Horses.*

Blanca's canter slowed. The air around Elen was distinctly hotter. The light through her eyelids was piercingly bright. She smelled dust and heat and something sharp and pungent that had a distinct aura of green. She opened her eyes.

This was not Hesperia, unless Hesperia had gone to desert since Elen last heard of it. These pastures were not even slightly green. The trees that dotted them were low and gnarled. Mountains rose steep and jagged above them to an achingly blue sky.

CHAPTER 2

Elen tumbled off Blanca's back into the shock of cold water. The mare finished the shrug that had rid her of her rider, blew a ripe snort, and lowered her head to drink. Her amusement was strong enough to taste. So was her satisfaction. She was frankly smug.

Elen sat up spluttering and spitting. Blanca had dropped her into a round steel tank. The water at least was clean, which had not always been Elen's experience of water tanks in pastures.

There was a spigot at one end of the tank, with a float on it that, when pressed down, sent fresh water pouring into the tank. She tipped her head to catch the flow, drinking in long, blissful swallows. She made herself stop before she took sick: not easy, as parched as she was, but she had that much sense at least.

She climbed out of the tank. Her clothes were dripping wet. She stripped off her coat in a fit of sudden panic. The leather outside was soaked, but the pocket inside was still dry. She heaved a sigh of relief. Her book was safe.

Then finally she had time to look around her. This had the feel of a sane and solid world and not a province of Faerie. A fierce yellow sun shone overhead, and the ground held steady underfoot.

Which of the many worlds it was, Elen could not tell, except that she was fairly sure it was not Hesperia. It most certainly was not Ymbria.

While Elen fished herself out of the tank, Blanca had wandered off into the herd. Elen could feel her inside, warm and quiet and present, but the physical Blanca was cropping dry sun-browned grass next to a red-roan mare who was almost as big as she was.

She was not a stranger here. Maybe she visited this world often, so that the horses knew her. Maybe—

Maybe she belonged here. But if this was where she came from, then this hot dry pasture was part of Earth, and Elen had come to the exact place she had been running away from.

Elen fought down the first, instinctive urge to flee back to the worldroad. She had learned her lesson.

Not without Blanca—and Blanca had brought her here.

"Blanca," Elen said. Her voice was faint, but the big white ear tilted toward her. "Blanca, we need to leave. This isn't where I wanted to go."

Blanca ignored her. She was busy eating, and then she would want to drink, and after that she thought she might ask her big red friend to scratch the itchy place just in front of her withers.

"I can do that," Elen said as a plan unfolded in her head. She walked up to Blanca. Blanca turned just so, to make it easier for Elen to reach. Elen rubbed and scratched until Blanca's neck stretched out and her upper lip wiggled in bliss.

"Now you can have your drink," Elen said, "and then we can go. Don't you think it's awfully hot here? Hesperia is much cooler. And there's grass—real grass, green and sweet."

Blanca turned her back on Elen. Elen stared at the massive hindquarters that were as tall as she was. She could scratch Blanca's tail, Blanca let her know, or she could go away and do what she was supposed to. Blanca was staying here. This was where she belonged.

There was no budging her. Blanca was exactly where she was supposed to be. And so, she made it clear, was Elen.

Elen spun away from her. The rest of the herd was paying no attention. Even the babies were busy eating or sleeping or basking in the sun.

Maybe one of the other mares would take Elen away from this place. They were all worldrunners. Elen had always been able to tell. It was a feeling under her skin, and a look they had to her eye, as if they were just a little more real than the world around them.

These were all mares, and some had foals at side. Those who did not had foals inside: heavy, swaying bellies and a distinctively placid and peaceful look.

Elen had been so focused on being in the wrong place and needing to get out of it that she had not even been thinking about what it meant that she was in a pasture full of pregnant mares and nursing mares and one frustrating, exasperating, completely treacherous and untrustworthy mare who was paying her no attention at all. Now finally her mind caught up with her eyes and her temper—and her heart did its best to stop.

If Elen was right, these were the most valuable horses there were. She stood where kings and chieftains would have killed to stand. The farms and ranches where Earth bred worldrunners were the most heavily guarded places in any world. No one could get near the mares or the foals. No person or power not of Earth could so much as look at them.

Yet here she was, a runaway from Ymbria, with

worldrunner mares and their foals all around her. No one had come running out of the barn on the rise above her, and no protections, magical or physical, had come roaring down upon her.

That was because of Blanca. The mare was still ignoring Elen, but she was grazing closer by, and her ear was tilted toward Elen. Blanca had brought her. Blanca protected her. That was why she was safe.

"I'm *not* safe!" Elen snapped at her. "I'm not even supposed to be here!"

Yes, you are.

Those were words, as clear and cold in Elen's head as if her own mother had spoken them. Blanca's head was up and her ears were aimed straight at Elen. Words, she let Elen know, were beneath her dignity, but so at the moment was Elen. This was Earth. Elen belonged on Earth. Blanca had brought her here. And that, Blanca declared with a stamp and a flattening of ears, was that.

The big grey mare looked nothing at all like Elen's tall and beautiful mother with her waving black hair and her warm brown skin, but when it came to making sure Elen did the last thing in any world that she wanted to do, they were exactly alike. "I hate you," Elen said. In that moment, she meant it with all her heart.

Blanca did not care in the slightest. The barn was that way, the slant of her ear said. Elen was to go there. Blanca had done what she came to Ymbria to do—and a long and unnecessarily complicated mess Elen had made of it, too.

That stung. Elen turned her back on the mare. If she could have kicked Blanca, or dropped a load of manure in that long smug face, she would have.

The sun beat down on her head. The heat sucked away her stubbornness. Whatever else she did, she had to get into the shade.

As she trudged sullenly toward the barn, some of the foals followed, curious. One curly-eared bay filly nipped at the hem of her shirt and danced away.

At any other time, in any other world, Elen could not have resisted stopping to play with the babies. Here, all she could do was promise to come back another time, and hope she could keep that promise.

There was nothing in the barn but dimness and quiet and relief from the heat. Horses dozed in some of the stalls, cooled by fans set in the sliding doors. The two on one side were even more pregnant than the mares in the pasture. The big bay horse on the other side of the aisle, asleep with his hip cocked and his head drooping, was obviously the stallion: he had the heavy neck and the broad jowls and the sheen that stallions have, even asleep.

He was aware of her. His little curly ear—so much

like the bay filly's that Elen knew whose daughter she was—bent as Elen passed by, but he never raised his head or challenged her.

"Well," she said to him, "that's trust. I'm honored, I think. Or maybe I should be insulted?"

His head drooped even lower. He began to snore.

A short bark of laughter escaped before Elen could stop it. She hurried on past him. After the brief reprieve of shade and relative coolness, the sun and heat at the other end of the aisle were a physical shock. Ymbria in summer could easily rival this ferocious, furnace heat, but she had come from Ymbria in winter; her body was adapted to snow and cold and ice-edged winds. She flinched back into the shade of the barn.

Through the eye-searing dazzle of sunlight she saw a flat sandy yard bordered on one side by a copse of low scrubby trees and on the other by a row of paddocks. Another barn stood across from her.

It was taller and wider than the one she had just passed through. Over its door hung the last sign she wanted to see: the swoop of a mountain's peak, and above it a nine-pointed star.

This was the House of the Star. The worldrunner had brought her straight to it.

"No," Elen said to the vision of Blanca that was still inside her head. "Oh, no. Not here. Of all possible places, not here."

She sprinted from the barn's dimness through

blinding light into the green shade of the grove. The track ran straight through it, sharp-edged with sunlight.

Blanca stood at the end of it like a white wall.

"Get out of my way," Elen said. She shaped each word carefully and edged it with ice.

Nothing cold could last in this horrible heat. Blanca stood perfectly still. She had nothing to say to Elen at all.

Elen darted around her—and ran straight into her. Everywhere Elen turned, Blanca was there. The whole world, every world, was full of her.

Only one road lay open. That was the road to Earth.

"*Not* if I can help it," Elen said through clenched teeth. She closed her eyes, squeezing them tight against the merciless sunlight of this place, and put her whole heart and soul into the vision of Hesperia that had opened up the worldroad.

Even there, Blanca would not let her be. Elen had not opened the worldroad, she said inside Elen's head. Blanca had. It was all Blanca, every bit of it—except the part where Elen had wandered off the road. That was Elen's fault. She was very clear about that.

"Why, thank you," Elen said, dripping sarcasm. While Blanca basked in smugness, Elen darted past her into the dazzle of light.

CHAPTER 3

A hammer of heat struck Elen hard enough to knock her to her knees. She looked up toward a roof of bare, spiny branches and around her at a tumble of green things. Directly in front of her, a stone fountain trickled into a basin. Carved in the stone was the symbol of mountain and star. She was still, in spite of everything she had done or tried, in the House of the Star.

She might laugh, or she might cry. Blanca's smugness was as thick around her as the heat. She threw fury back at it, envisioning jets of flame. They rolled harmlessly off that shining white coat.

A voice spoke behind her. "Hello! Where did you come from?"

Elen whipped around. A girl about her own age was standing just inside the shelter. She was tall and narrow, with coppery-colored hair braided tightly out of her face, and a splendid crop of freckles. She was dressed in what must be the manner of Earth: stiff dark-blue trousers with a lighter blue shirt tucked into them, and shiny brown boots with pointed toes.

"You must have just got here," the girl said. She was speaking one of the languages of Earth. Elen had learned it because she wanted to be a worldrider. It had been one more reason that her mother chose her for this.

There was no answer in Elen's head now. She was too tangled up with shock and anger and resistance that did her no good no matter how hard she tried. All she could do was stare at the redheaded girl.

The girl stared back. It was a very intense stare, and it made Elen rather uncomfortable. She felt as if she was being judged, and not especially kindly, either.

The girl seemed to come to a decision, or else to remember the manners she had been taught. She thrust out a hand. "Ria," she said.

That must be her name. Elen's mind was not working well at all. She kept her hands to herself, but she managed to say, "Elen."

"Elen," Ria repeated. "You're in the cabin on the end. I saw your name on the door."

"Thank you," said Elen, "but I'm not staying. If you'd be so kind as to show me the way out, I'll not trouble you further."

Ria frowned as if puzzled. "You *are* Elen with one 'L,' aren't you? If that's not you and you belong to one of the other campers, everybody's gone who isn't part of camp. The last run to town left an hour ago."

"Camp?" Elen asked. "I'm not sure I—"

"Horse camp at Rancho Estrella," said Ria. "That's what we're all here for. You missed the barn tour; now you'll have to wait till morning to meet the horses."

In spite of everything, Elen's heart leaped. Horses, riding, the House of the Star—all her childhood dreams were here, now. And there seemed to be no way to get out of it.

No, there is not, Blanca said inside her head: actual words, as clear as if the mare had spoken aloud.

Elen had nothing to say to her, except one word, the worst word an Ymbrian knew. *Traitor.*

Blanca did not even bother to laugh. She was much too pleased with her own cleverness, and much too busy eating her dinner.

Elen spoke through that wave of smugness. "Yes, it seems I am here for camp. It also seems that I'm late. Is there someone to whom I should present myself?"

"That would be Megan," Ria said. "Come on. I'll show you where to go."

If this was as treacherous a guide as Blanca had been, Elen was in serious trouble. But what other choice did she have? She was completely alone here. Ria seemed to be one of those people who takes charge without even thinking about it, and manages everyone and everything with relentless efficiency.

Elen was used to being one of those people. It was a new experience to be taken in hand and managed by someone who was not her mother.

Elen was in the enemy's camp—that was a useful word, though she doubted it meant the same thing to Ria as it did to her. She took care to study the world around her and the people she met, the better to defend herself against them.

Ria led her across a wide sandy courtyard surrounded by a brown brick wall. The space within was dotted with bits of fierce and spiky greenery. Flowers tumbled over the walls and coiled up posts and pillars, bright red and orange and purple against the brown of wood or stone or brick. Paths of sand lined with stones ran in a circle around the square and in spokes toward the center, where stood the shelter of wooden posts and narrow spiny branches into which Blanca had flung Elen.

Most of the buildings around the square were rather small, but on each side was a larger one. The house on the right had its own wall, but Ria led Elen to the other, which, as if in contrast, had a broad, open porch. The door was wide, and though it was closed to keep the heat out, it opened easily to Ria's touch.

It was beautifully cool inside, and so dim it was almost dark after the sun's glare. Elen stood on a floor of tiles the color of red earth, blinking until her eyes focused.

A room opened in front of her, all wood and stone and leather. It had an interesting smell, a little like saddles and horses and a little like the desert heat. There were benches and couches and chairs and odd bits of tables and cabinets, and a stone fireplace big enough to roast an ox in.

The far wall was all of glass. It looked out across a wooden porch and a sharp-spined garden to an expanse of sand and scrub and stony foothills rising up to the jagged teeth of mountains.

Elen had been born in gentler country, but as she stood there, full of rebellion and anger and crushing exhaustion, something about those mountains and that desert and that sky lodged in her heart. Her skin stung from the sun and itched with dryness, and yet it felt wonderful.

She hardly noticed that there were people in the room, until Ria called out beside her and made her jump like a cat. "Megan! Here's another one."

Half a dozen faces turned toward them. Elen only had energy to pay attention to the one who stepped out of the crowd. Megan looked like an older version of Ria: tall and milky-skinned, with a long red-gold braid. Maybe they were related.

"This is Elen," Ria said. "She's lost, I think. She says she needs a ride home."

That was not what Elen had said, but it was close enough to the truth that she did not try to correct it. Megan was studying her; she kept her back straight and her chin up, like a soldier at inspection.

After a moment that seemed to stretch into an hour, Megan turned to speak to the rest. "If you don't mind, everybody, I'll take Elen into the office and get her signed in. Sara, show them how the kitchen works. I'll be back in a bit."

She rounded up Elen with a glance. She was good: Elen bowed to her talent, though the gesture nearly made her fall over. She was fading fast—and that, she could not afford to do.

She scraped herself together and followed Megan away from all the staring eyes and curious faces.

The office was a small room down the hall from the common room, windowless and cluttered, with a desk crowded into the middle, and two chairs: one behind the desk and one in front of it. There were books everywhere, and metal cabinets between and around the shelves.

Megan shut the door. Elen did not hear the click of a lock, but she was by no means reassured. When Megan sat behind the desk, Elen stayed on her feet. "This is a mistake," she said. "I'm not supposed to be here."

"Really?" said Megan. "According to the camp list, you are."

Elen's temper finally snapped. "Camp? What is this camp? Camp of war? Camp for a caravan? What?"

Megan lifted an eyebrow at the outburst, but it did not ruffle her calm at all. "Officially, it's riders' camp at Rancho Estrella. Young people come to ride and learn about horses, live on the ranch, and in this season, brag that they survived summer in southern Arizona. We have sessions all year round, but this one is special. Campers in this session are here to prove that they're suited for the ranch's other purpose besides hosting guests and breeding cow horses."

"Ending wars between worlds?"

"That's part of it," Megan said. "We don't talk about it on this side of the ranch."

"This side?" Elen was losing her grip again. It was getting harder and harder to pull herself back into focus. "I don't know what you're talking about. I don't know anything but that I refused to come here. I still refuse. I want to leave."

"Do you?"

Megan looked straight into her eyes. Elen did her best to stare straight back, though it felt as if she was being taken apart from the inside out. It was a great deal like crossing wills with Blanca.

"You're a worldrider," Elen said.

"We don't talk about that here, either," said Megan. "Earth isn't like anywhere else. Most of it knows nothing about the roads or the worlds they lead to, and much of the rest doesn't believe they're real. Rancho Estrella lives in both worlds. This half is in Earth; it's a guest ranch and a horse ranch, and nobody who comes here from outside needs to know what the other half is. That's the rule for camp. You don't talk about its real purpose, and you don't tell people where you come from. You don't pass the gate into the other half, either, until you've earned the right to do it. That means being accepted into the worldriders' school. Camp is your entrance exam. The rest of the campers are the class you'll move on with—or else they'll fall short and be sent home."

Elen heard all of that, and some made sense and

some was completely new to her. But none of it mattered, because it was not real. "I don't believe you," she said. "Everybody knows that if someone from the worlds that aren't Earth is chosen to be a worldrider, he goes straight into one of the schools. There isn't any test. He just goes. I'm not getting that far because I'm not a recruit. I'm a hostage."

"I suppose you are," Megan said, which made Elen even angrier.

"I don't know or care what game I'm expected to play," she said. "I won't play it. I want to go home. I demand that you send me home."

She tried to keep her voice level, but it insisted on spiraling upward. Megan winced, but she was no more movable than Blanca had been. "That's too bad," she said, "for Ymbria, considering what will happen if you refuse to play, as you put it. And for you, because the worldrunners believe that you could be a rider. You have a great deal to learn, they say, but you understand the roads rather well, for a human child."

"The worldrunners believe?" said Elen. "The *worldrunners* say? They're horses!"

"So they are," Megan said. "You are just as stubborn as your mother warned us you would be. She sent you a message. She said, 'If you absolutely insist on coming home, we will take you. But everything that happens after that will be on your head.'"

Those words were like a blow to Elen's center. For a terribly long count of seconds, she could not even remember how to breathe.

Megan did not try to win her over with sympathy. "You'll have to stay the night: we can't spare anyone to take you back before tomorrow. Maybe by then you'll change your mind. I gather that has been known to happen?"

Elen's eyes narrowed. "I'll stay," she said, "if you'll promise me something. Swear by whatever you hold allegiance to that I won't be forced to marry the boy from Caledon. That's what it's all supposed to be for, isn't it? Tell me the truth now. No more lies."

Megan's expression was as bland as ever, but Elen could swear that her eyes had broken out in laughter. "You will not be forced to marry the one who was sent from Caledon. That I can promise you. All we ask is that you live together, work together, and refrain from killing each other."

"I don't know if either of us can do that," Elen said.

"You will try," said Megan with an edge of steel.

"I will try," Elen agreed grudgingly. It was the safest thing she could say, and it cost her little in the end. She had sworn no oath. Nor would she. She refused to be bound here for any reason.

Megan's glance was full of doubts. But she said, "Be sure you follow the rules. Stay on this side of the ranch, say nothing about anything or anyone on the other side, and—"

"Or what?" Elen demanded. "What happens if I don't?"

"You're expelled," said Megan. "You go back home. You can never come back."

That was exactly what Elen told herself she wanted—but if she did, it would be the end of Ymbria. Megan had made that perfectly clear. So, in her message, had Elen's mother.

"I don't want to," Elen said. "I hate that I have to. But I don't have a choice, do I?"

"You always have a choice," Megan said. She stood up. "Welcome to Rancho Estrella. John David will be speaking with you this evening before dinner. He apologizes for not being here to greet you, and hopes that you'll forgive him."

Elen knew that name. Everyone along the world-roads did. John David was the master of this house, and a great power among the worlds. She was here because of him.

Training made her say, "Of course I forgive him." Everything else she had endured so far made her add, "At least for that."

Was that a sigh? Megan was back to her expressionless self again; it was hard to tell. "Come with me," she said, "and try to pretend that you want to be here. Everyone else does, very much."

"Well," said Elen, "so would I, if it weren't for the boy from Caledon."

Megan looked as if she might have said something about that, but thought better of it. She shook her head instead, and took Elen back out for a proper meeting with the rest of the campers.

CHAPTER 4

There was no boy from Caledon—at least not in the group of campers that gathered in the lounge. All of them were from Earth. Elen was the only one from anywhere else.

That, she had not expected. After she got over wanting to hit Megan for leading her on and letting her think he was there, Elen started to feel slightly better about this trap she had fallen into. Had the Caledonian refused to come to Earth, too, but had the luck or the sense to stay off the worldroads and away from the likes of Blanca? Or had he tried and died, as Elen almost had?

That would be a wonderful thing. Because if he was not here and Elen still could not go back to Ymbria, that meant her life here would be very much different. Rancho Estrella with a Caledonian in it was unbearable. Rancho Estrella without him was Elen's dream.

She clamped down hard on the surge of excitement. There must still be a price for her presence, some difficult or painful thing she had to do. Maybe it was no more and no less than passing whatever tests there were and being accepted into the worldriders' school.

She could do that. Nothing in the worlds would make her happier.

The rest of that afternoon passed in a blur. There was a great deal to do and know: in the kitchen, in the library that filled the second story of the lodge, in the cabins and around the ranch, and above all in the barns—though that part, to Elen's disappointment, would wait until morning.

By the time the sun began to sink, the boys were running in a pack and the girls had slid together naturally, drawn to one another as horse girls always are. Elen liked the twins Lilly and Nan very much, but Ria and the girl named Sara struck her with something more: that thing she recognized as kinship. They were a tribe; they belonged together. It was a most peculiar feeling, and quite wonderful.

Most of the cabins around the square were meant for two, but the one on the end near the walled house, with the lemon tree in front, had space for three. Ria's name was on the door. So were Sara's and her own.

Lilly and Nan had the cabin next to theirs. The boys were across the square: Matt and Lucas together, and quiet brown-haired Nick in solitude—unless the coward from Caledon put in an appearance after all.

Elen could almost forget how hard she had fought not to come here. This was everything she had dreamed it would be, except horses—and they would have those first thing in the morning.

But first Elen had to face the master of the house. She was perfectly calm about that until Megan told her it was time. "He's in the ranch house," Megan said. "Through the gate to the door, and straight on down the hall."

"You're not coming?" Elen asked.

"He won't eat you," Megan said, not quite smiling.

Elen wondered about that, but she had not been born a coward. She crossed the square in heat that had risen to a breathless crescendo.

The wall around the ranch house opened into a courtyard with another fountain, of copper this time, and a wondrous surprise: a garden of roses. They were somewhat crisped by the heat, but they were thriving.

Elen loved roses. Her favorite place in her mother's palace, except for the stables, was the rose garden. She even slept there on fine nights in summer, surrounded by such a glory of color and fragrance that she could get dizzy just thinking about it. Finding it in this place made her terribly homesick, and yet it also reminded her of why she had to be here. "I'm doing this for Ymbria," she said to herself. "I have to remember that."

She paused to breathe in that sweetest of all scents and gather her courage. When she had as much of that as she was going to get, she slipped through the heavy wooden door.

The ranch house felt almost cold. Elen shivered. She was getting used to the double shock of cool and dim after hot and bright; she had already learned to pause and take time to adapt.

There was a door at the end of the hall, standing open. The room beyond was cluttered and comfortable, with a saddle on a wooden rack in the middle of the floor, and bridle parts in a pile on a worn and sagging couch.

A man sat on the couch with a sponge and saddle soap, cleaning a plain leather headstall. He looked like Sara with his straight black hair and narrow dark eyes, but his skin was redder and his cheekbones broader than hers, and he was built square and solid. His clothes were well worn; his boots looked as if they had traveled from one end of the worldroads to the other.

He could have passed for a stablehand, but Elen would never have made that mistake. She could feel the power in him: deep and quiet, the way a horseman's should be. This could only be the master of the House of the Star. She bowed to him as one should to a great lord of the worlds.

He nodded in return and laid the bridle aside. "Sit," he said, tilting his head toward a chair.

Elen would have been happier standing, but some invitations were not for refusing. She perched on the edge of the seat, folded her hands and tried to breathe quietly.

"We've sent word to your mother," John David said. "She knows you're safe."

"I guessed as much from what Megan said," Elen said. "Thank you."

It was hard to know what else to say. She settled on silence.

John David studied her. She hoped she passed muster. Her clothes were Earth clothes: one of the chests of drawers in the cabin had her name on it, and was full of shirts and trousers and boots and shoes and bits of this and that.

Sara had helped her dress in the blue trousers that she called *jeans*, with a crisp white shirt and a leather belt and pointed boots like Ria's. It was all new and stiff and not terribly comfortable, but it fit surprisingly well. Elen did not think she looked too terrible in it.

After a while John David said, "You'll have noticed that not all our plans have turned out as we expected— even with Blanca's help."

"What, that the boy from Caledon never came here after all?" Elen nodded. "I can't say I'm horribly disappointed."

"No?" John David stood. When she started to get up as well, he waved her back down. "Are you thirsty?"

"A little," she admitted. In truth it was more than a little: the air here was drier than any air of Ymbria.

"I'll get you something to drink," he said. "Wait here."

He was gone before she could object. She slid back in the big soft chair. Her fit of nerves had faded. Now she was simply curious. Was he going to tell her what had happened? Caledon must be in terrible trouble. She hoped so. No world deserved it more.

She could hear John David raising a clatter deeper in the house. The knock on the door at first seemed part of it, but when it sharpened, Elen realized what it was. Since there was no one else to do it, she said, "Come in."

It was Ria. She looked unwontedly white and tense; she would not meet Elen's eyes, though Elen welcomed her with a smile. Elen was more puzzled than ever. "I'm glad you're here," she said. "I was starting to feel horribly singled out. I'm not really, am I? He must talk to all the campers before the session starts."

Ria shook her head but said nothing. She seemed even more nervous than Elen had been, shifting from foot to foot and darting glances around the room.

"You should sit down," Elen said. "He said he'll be back directly."

Ria nodded tightly and stayed on her feet. She started to prowl, poking at books on shelves and tables, lifting and setting down a bronze horse, a globe of many-colored glass, a dragon's tooth that had turned to stone. She paused as she passed the window and stood too still, staring at the blood-red light of sunset on the mountains.

John David came in from the kitchen at last with a pitcher of water and a stack of cups—three of them. He filled each one.

Elen took hers and drank, because her throat was so dry it hurt. Ria stared at the one she was given, as if she had never seen either water or a cup before.

John David sat where he had been when Elen came in. He took a sip, set the cup on the table beside the sofa, and said, "Now, Ria."

Ria's shoulders went rigid. "You do it," she told the mountains.

"It's not mine to do," John David said.

Ria spun. "All right," she said with tightly reined-in fury. "All *right!*" Her eyes flashed to Elen. "I heard what you said about Caledon—what cowards and liars everyone is there. But it was you who ran away from duty and honor, not anyone from Caledon. A world-runner had to hunt you down and bring you here."

The force of her words rocked Elen back in the chair. Ria who felt like kin, Ria who shared a cabin and a tribe and a love of horses, was gone. This person who wore her face was downright furious, and openly scornful.

"I wasn't afraid!" Elen protested. "I just couldn't stand the thought of marrying a lying thief from Caledon."

"Why? Would you rather marry a sneaking coward from Ymbria?"

Elen sprang to her feet. She caught herself before she leaped. It was not sanity that stopped her. It was pure shock.

Those words, that face, even that accent, so much stronger now with temper—

"You're from Caledon," she said.

"And you're from Ymbria," Ria said, as if Elen were a very small and very stupid child.

"You're a *girl!*"

Ria's mouth twisted. "I am, aren't I?"

Elen wanted to gag. She had liked this person. She had thought they could be friends.

"Liar to the last," she said. Her voice was thick with revulsion. "You knew the moment you met me, didn't you? Did you think it was amusing to lead me on, smile and lie, and pretend you were from Earth?"

"Yes, I knew," Ria said. "You look just like your mother. I was brought up to be courteous to strangers, and not to judge anyone for good or ill until I'd come to know them. Obviously that's not the way in Ymbria."

"In Ymbria we know what Caledon is—over and over and over, for hundreds and hundreds of years. You never change. You're not capable of it."

Ria laughed, sharp enough to cut. "You would know. Wouldn't you? You're my cousin. I'm yours. You have as much blood of Caledon in you as I have of Ymbria. We've been marrying and remarrying and intermarrying for so long, we're all the same family."

"You are not my family," Elen said. She bit off each word as she spoke it. "No matter what blood is in me, I am *not* of Caledon."

"You are not," Ria agreed all too willingly. "Caledon has never bred a coward or a runaway. That's all Ymbria."

"Better a runaway than a liar! You didn't just pretend to be a friend. You pretended to be something even worse—my tribe. The tribe of girls who love horses."

"That is not a lie," Ria said. "I'm a girl. Horses are the most wonderful thing in any world. I want to be a worldrider."

"But you're not supposed to *be* here! You're supposed to be a boy!"

"Why?" said Ria.

Elen opened her mouth. There was no answer waiting for her, no word that immediately came to mind. She had to scramble to find any at all. "Why? Because it's always been a girl from Ymbria and a boy from Caledon. It's tradition."

"Our whole war is tradition," Ria said. "Isn't it time we broke it?"

"I think it's rather brilliant," John David said.

His voice was mild, his expression calmly interested. He met each scorching glare with the faintest hint of a smile. "Think about it," he said. "Ymbria's emissary has no desire to marry a Caledonian. In the meantime Caledon noticed that there was nothing in the treaty to require that their contribution be male. So they sent a daughter who happens to love horses. All those marriages have done nothing but make the hatred worse. A pair of horse girls already have common ground, something they both love more than anything. Isn't that what's been lacking? A place in the heart for the old enemies to truly and finally meet?"

"That wasn't why my family did it," Ria said.

"But they did," said John David.

"You mean they outsmarted themselves?" Elen asked. "They do that. For people who make such an outcry about honor, they're as dishonorable as any creatures living."

"No!" said Ria. "I'm not like that. My father and uncles aren't, either. They just couldn't face giving up another son to a lost cause."

"So they gave up a daughter." Elen's head hurt; there was a sour taste in her mouth. "They must really want to get rid of you."

"No more than your mother does you," Ria said.

"She wanted me to have horses," Elen said, "and keep Ymbria from being cut off from the worldroads."

"Yes," Ria said. "All we have to do is stay here, be polite to each other, and do as we're told. As long as we do that, our worlds get to stay alive. *I'm* strong enough to do that if I have to. But you're not. Are you? You'll keep this war going till we're all dead and gone."

"*We're* not the ones who started it."

"And we're not the ones who've kept it going for twice a thousand years!"

Elen sucked in a breath, forcing herself to be calm. To see straight. To think. "That's it," she said. "Enough. I'm done. I don't care how hard you try: I'm not playing your game."

"So you're going home?" Ria demanded.

Elen bit her tongue. She could say yes, she was going—then make John David send her back to Ymbria. That was why she was here.

And yet, in front of this girl from Caledon, she heard herself say, "No. I'm here honestly, the way I'm supposed to be."

"Because a worldrunner forced you to," said Ria.

"I'm staying," said Elen. "If you want to go, go."

"Not likely," Ria said.

They glared at each other. Elen for one was ready to slap her. No way in any world was she going to let herself be friends with a Caledonian.

CHAPTER 5

"Why do you hate Ria so much?" asked Sara.

Dinner had been miserable, at least for Elen. They all had to eat together in the lodge, at one of the long, polished tables in the dining room. When Ria sat at one end, Elen pointedly chose the other.

She hardly noticed what she ate. None of it was terribly strange: roast fowl, baked roots, leafy green things in a salad, and a cold sweet that was remarkably good. Sara called it "ice cream." Elen might have tasted it with more attention if she had not had to sit at the same table with her worst enemy.

Ria kept glaring at her down the length of the table. Elen surrounded herself with icy silence. Everybody else tried to act as if nothing was happening, but it was too obvious that something was.

"Wow," Elen heard Matt say to Lilly. "It's like Arabs and Israelis."

"Cats and dogs," Lilly said.

"Sharks and swimmers," said Lucas.

"Oh, sure," said Lilly, "but who's the shark?"

After dinner they scattered to their cabins. That meant, for Elen, that she had to go to the cabin she shared with the Caledonian.

She was not going to move out. Ria was supposed to be in Nick's cabin. She could go there and leave Elen alone.

Elen pulled her bedding off the bunk above Ria's and dragged it into the outer room. The couch was lumpy and hard, but it had walls and a door between it and Ria.

Sara cornered her there. "Why do you hate her? You never even met her before today."

"She's from Caledon," Elen said.

Sara raised her eyebrows. "So?"

"So? We've been at war for almost as long as worldrunners have been traveling the roads."

"Good reason to end it, then, I would think," said Sara.

"There *is* no end," Elen said. "It's been going on so long, with so many lives lost or broken and so many battles and so much anger and grief and hate that there isn't any way to fix it. I don't know why anybody even tries."

"Because if we don't, all the worlds will keep getting the fallout." Sara looked straight into Elen's face. "You've never left Ymbria before, have you? You haven't seen what happens when your worlds have one of their battles that spills over to half a dozen other worlds, or when some of your people go hunting each other from world to world. Other people get hurt. Too often they die. Worlds take damage, sometimes so badly that they can't survive."

Sara stopped to breathe. This mattered to her—deeply. As if she had a personal stake in it. She looked as if she wanted to cry, but anger had burned all the tears away.

Elen wanted to say something, anything, to deny that what Sara said was true. But it was. Even in Ymbria, Elen had known that.

"That's why you're here," Sara said. "That fight you had last year with Caledon, that raged all the way down the worldroads to Tirnan and Oghan, left Tirnan a wasteland and stripped all the magic out of Oghan: it wasn't the first time such a thing happened. It has to be the last. Otherwise there won't be anybody left, on or off the roads."

"*We* didn't start the war," Elen said.

"It wouldn't have *been* a war if Ymbria hadn't cut and run when it should have stood and fought," Ria said from the door.

"Ymbria *didn't* run!" Elen flared back at her. She turned her back on Ria and said to Sara, "Before the worldrunners came, Ymbria and Caledon were allies. We had found a way to travel the worldroads using talismans wrought of magic and of silver. Caledon was rich in silver. We traded for the metal and taught its people how to use the talismans, and between us we grew rich in trade and power.

"Then the worldrunners came. Our talismans weren't terribly hard to use if a person knew their secret, but they were not easy or simple to make. That made them rare and costly, and they could only protect one or two people at a time. Travel on the worldroads was difficult and expensive, and the Guides as we called them became very wealthy. Worldrunners ended all that. One or two of them could escort a whole caravan, and bring it safe to the place where it wanted to go.

"That was a great blow to our worlds," Elen said. "All the other worlds stopped paying us to transport their treasures. Caledon's king and our queen had a council, and they agreed that they had to do something. Worldrunners then were not numerous at all, and they only lived in one place, on a cold and misty island in the north of Earth."

"Wales," Sara said. "Gwynedd, it was then."

"Gwynedd," Elen said. "Yes. The council decided to destroy the horses and the place and everyone on it, get rid of them completely—"

"Ymbria wanted that," Ria interrupted. "Caledon wanted to capture the worldrunners instead, and take control of them. Nobody knew then that worldrunners will only breed or foal on Earth."

"Ymbria knew," Elen said. "Our queen was a seer. She saw the truth. Your king refused to believe her, but some of his people had more sense. They all agreed to destroy instead of capture. But when they mounted the attack on Earth, they found that it was defended. The powers of Faerie were fighting for it. The Horned King himself rode out against them. Then Caledon turned traitor. It betrayed Ymbria to the enemy, and bought its own safety with the lives and souls of its allies."

"That's not true!" Ria said fiercely. "Ymbria's army saw the Wild Hunt coming and broke and ran. Caledon was captured, though it fought to a standstill, and forced to surrender. For that it won clemency. But Ymbria had run away, and it paid the price for its cowardice. It was sentenced to be cut off from the worldroads. But Caledon spoke for it, and won it a reprieve.

It tried to save your sorry nation. And what did it get in return? Endless war and festering resentment."

"You betrayed us." Elen thrust the words at her, hoping they stabbed deep. "You always betray us."

Ria bared her teeth. "Oh, do we? Tell Sara why you really hate us. Go on, tell her."

Elen's throat locked shut. She could not have spoken if she had wanted to.

Ria had no such failing. "This isn't just an ancient and traditional hatred," she said to Sara. "It's personal. It's her own father she hates—because he was one of us."

"He was not my father! He seduced my mother after my real father died. He forced her to marry him, and then abandoned her when I was born. He never wanted me. He only wanted her because she was a prize to brag about: the poor widowed queen of Ymbria, fallen all into a flutter over a pair of handsome eyes and a lying smile."

"That's not even half true," Ria said. "You were born a full year after he saw your mother in the high courts of Faerie, speaking for her people, and fell in love—and she fell in love with him. He was wise and kind and honorable, and he adored her. People even said they might bring an end to the war at last, because it was no cold marriage of state but a true love match. But there were those in Ymbria who had no desire to end the war. They loved conflict too much, and were drunk on the taste of blood. They lured him out on a hunt one day, telling tales of a wild boar that was ravaging the villages. But there was no boar. He rode into an ambush. They killed him. He didn't abandon you, you selfish little fool. He died. Do you know what his last words were? 'Tell my lady and my daughter that I love them both with all my heart.' "

Tears were streaming down Elen's face. "You're lying. There's no way you can know any such thing. He went out hunting and never came back. He ran away to Caledon and left my mother to grieve. He never even said good-bye."

"He never said good-bye because he never meant to leave either of you. He was my mother's brother. She has the gift of far seeing. She saw him die. She heard what he said. She tried to send the message to your mother, but the people who wanted him dead were on watch against just such a thing. They made sure she never knew. But we did. *We* know who killed Midir of Caer Goch."

"No," said Elen. "I don't believe you. Maybe some of our people did kill him—but he did something to deserve it."

"He was from Caledon," Ria said. "That was all the crime he ever needed to commit."

"Yes!" Elen spat at her. "*Yes!*"

"That's it," Sara said. She pushed Ria back into the

bedroom and shut the door in her face. Before Elen could thank her for choosing the right side, she spun and lashed out. "*Don't* say a word. If you're going to re-fight every battle of the past two thousand years, go right ahead. But not here and not now and not while I have to be in the middle."

"But—" Elen said.

"No," said Sara. "Not a word." She pushed the inside door open. "You, too," she said to Ria. "You can do whatever you like out there, or whatever Megan or Uncle John will let you get away with. In here, nobody fights. Everybody keeps quiet and swears a truce."

Elen growled. Ria muttered to herself in gutter Caledonian, which Elen was sorry to admit she knew. Sara pinned them both with her glare. "Swear."

Neither wanted to be the first to give in. Sara was half a head shorter than either of them and could have weighed no more than a bird, but she managed to loom over them. "Do I have to knock your heads together?"

"No," Elen said sullenly. At the same time, Ria shook her head, scowling.

"We swear," they said in chorus.

They both recoiled, appalled, but Sara was satisfied. "Good. You can start now. We're all sleeping in the same room, and we're going to be nice about it. If you can't stand each other, at least be polite."

"Who *are* you?" Elen demanded.

"I'm the person who has to put up with both of you," Sara said. "Here, I'll help you move back in."

Elen started to dig in her heels. But then it occurred to her that if Ria had Sara to herself, she could win her over with that lying Caledonian tongue. Then Elen would have two enemies in the cabin instead of one.

She had better have them both where she could watch them. It was humiliating to have to undo her grand exit, but it was worth the embarrassment to see how unhappy Ria was about it. If Elen had to be miserable, everyone else should, too.

The tears came after the lights were out, when no one else could see. Elen lay in a strange bed in a strange world full of smells she had never smelled before, surrounded by people and places that would never be her own. Her enemy slept in the bed beneath her—which at least was a kind of justice.

What Ria had said about Elen's father—Elen did not want to believe it. Not now, not ever. She had lived most of her life hating him. She was not going to give it up because of anything a Caledonian said.

She dried her eyes on the sheet and buried her face in the pillow. The clean cloth smell of it melted into the sweet, pungent smell of horse.

She could feel the warm neck against her cheek, and hear the deep slow breathing in her ear. It was Blanca. She would know that neck and that rhythm of breath in any world.

She should be furious, but that was like being angry at her own heart. In her half-dream, she wrapped her arms around the big white neck. It curved to embrace her, and Blanca whickered, as gentle as a mare with her foal.

Then, in spite of everything, Elen could sleep.

CHAPTER 6

Morning began early, just as the sun was coming up. Elen woke with the memory of Blanca's presence still wrapped around her. It made the sight of Ria almost bearable, and let her face breakfast with something approaching interest.

She knew eggs and bacon. Two things were completely new: a glorious golden liquid called orange juice, and something that looked like a dreadful mash of indecipherable ingredients, but was a fiery delight on the tongue. There was a kind of flat bread in it, and eggs and cheese, and something bright and fierce called salsa, all mixed in together. It was wonderful. She made Sara repeat what it was called. *"Chilaquiles."*

She loved the sound of that. When everyone had eaten and Megan had herded them out into heat that was already breathtaking, Elen repeated the word to herself. *Chilaquiles. Chilaquiles.* She hoped there would be more tomorrow, both for the taste and for the chance to say the word again.

Meanwhile there was something much more wonderful ahead of her: they were going to see the horses.

Elen expected to be led to the barns and pastures she had seen the day before, but Megan took them down a dusty path to a different place. Here were bare brown pastures, too, and groves of low, spiky trees, and one tall sand-colored barn backed up against a long and wide arena. Down along the sides of the arena stood rows of metal roofs with metal pipe stalls under them, and horses.

These were not worldrunners. Campers had to earn those by proving that they had the mind and the skill to handle their mortal cousins. But they were horses of Earth, and that was magic enough.

They were all colors and sizes, from big feathered-legged draft horses that Megan called the Clydes, to a tiny pony in a corner stall, no taller than one of the ranch dogs. And of course there were riding horses, more than Elen could stop to count.

The campers tried to scatter, as dizzy with the delight of it all as Elen was, but Megan reined them in. "You'll get to know every horse here," she said, "and clean its stall, too. But first we have a test for you."

That stopped them short. Matt went white, which won him loud mockery from his brother. "This isn't school, dumbhead. Nobody can throw you out if you flunk."

"No?" said someone new.

He had been leaning on the fence for a while, but nobody had bothered to notice, because there were horses to look at first. He wore what seemed to be the uniform here, battered boots and well-worn jeans and a serviceable shirt, with a straw hat to shade his head from the sun.

He looked almost Ymbrian, with his curly black hair and dark eyes, but somehow he looked like John David, too. He had an easy grace about him, though he must not be much older than Megan, and an air of being very sure of who he was and what he was and why he was there.

"This is Bran," Megan said, "and you'll get to know each other very well: he's in charge of the horse part of horse camp. While you're in the barns, you'll be doing whatever he asks you to do. And yes, Lucas, he can throw you out."

Lucas flushed and stuttered, but no one had time to laugh at him. While Megan spoke, one of the stablehands had led a saddled and bridled horse into the arena. The saddle reminded Elen somewhat of knights' saddles in Ymbria: high before and behind, though the horn in front was strange, and so was the lack of bit to the bridle.

"No bit?" Elen asked.

"That's a bosal," Sara said. "You get to ride with a bit after you prove you've got the hands for it."

People had to prove everything here, Elen thought as she watched Bran take the reins and pause to stroke the sleek chestnut neck, murmuring in the horse's ear. *That* was a horseman. She sighed to see it. So, she happened to notice, did all the other girls—including Ria.

That concentrated Elen's mind wonderfully. Anything Ria wanted, Elen could find a way to use against her.

Bran turned from the horse who was so clearly a friend, and scanned all their faces. His eye lit on Lucas; he smiled a remarkably sweet smile. "Before you can ride on this ranch, you have a test to pass. I'll start with you. Come and meet Max."

Lucas had his cockiness back. He sauntered forward and stopped just a little too close to Bran, which let him tower impressively over the much shorter man.

Bran's smile grew, if possible, even sweeter. "Remember what Megan said. Do what I ask, and you'll do well. Here, take the reins. Show me how you mount."

Lucas might be an idiot, but he was no fool. He made sure the cinch was tight and the stirrups were the right length before he mounted the gelding. Max stood patiently while he did that, keeping an ear tilted toward Bran and an eye on the stranger.

Finally Lucas satisfied himself that there was no trickery with the tack. He mounted easily and paused, taking his time again. Max offered no objection.

Neither did Bran. He nodded, but his eyes were watchful. "Now walk," he said.

Lucas did as he was told. Max was big, taller than Blanca but much narrower, and he seemed a little lazy. He plodded docilely in a circle around Bran, first in a walk and then in a shuffling jog.

Elen began to understand what the test was. Lucas could ride; there was no mistaking that. The longer he went on, the more visibly bored he became, riding patterns and changes of gait as Bran instructed. He slouched a little more with each turn and transition, and looked as if he was fighting to swallow a yawn.

At last Bran allowed him to shift from jog to lope. That gait, too, was low and lackluster, barely managing to stay shy of four beats instead of the proper three. When Bran called for a figure eight, Lucas saw an opening.

Elen was half asleep herself by then. She saw Lucas clamp heels to the gelding's sides, and Max's head go down and his ears go flat. There was a blur; then Lucas hit the dirt, and Max threw in one last buck-and-kick before trotting over to Bran.

Lucas left the field with a mouthful of sand and nothing broken but his dignity. No one had any sympathy to spare.

Nobody laughed, either. Nobody dared.

Bran caught Matt's eye, though Lucas' brother did his best to shrink down and make himself invisible, and held out the reins. Matt came forward warily. Max had returned to his former self again, like an old plow horse with flopping ears and sagging lower lip. While Matt followed Bran's instructions exactly, the gelding offered perfect obedience—and when Bran asked for a lope, Matt sat very, very still and rode very, very carefully.

The rest of them had learned the lesson well. They all rode well, too. No one here was a novice.

Elen kept waiting to be called, but Bran seemed determined to ignore her. Max tested the three boys and Lilly, then went out to pasture for a well-deserved roll and a long drink of water. A smaller horse took his place, a pretty blue roan with a scattering of black spots over the hips.

"This is Chica," Bran said. The mare stood next to him with her little lean ears pricked, bright-eyed and alert, pawing lightly as he ran his eyes over the campers who were still left to test. "Nan," he said to the quieter of the twin sisters.

She came out of the line willingly enough, introduced herself to Chica by offering her hand to be sniffed, and mounted in a quick, light sweep.

"Bet you a quarter she goes rodeo inside of five minutes," Matt said to Lucas.

"My money's on her going racehorse instead," Nick said, tossing a silvery coin in the brothers' direction.

Lucas plucked it out of the air with a grin. "Done!" he said.

Nan picked up the reins. Chica was in motion already, dancing forward.

"Ooh, hot one," Lucas said. He sounded impressed.

Nick nodded. "Rusher. She won't buck. She'll run."

Elen agreed with Nick. Chica reminded her of Brychan. She had the same expression, and the same air of not just wanting to go fast, but loving it.

Nan was a good rider. But in Chica's clear opinion, she had a great deal to learn. As soon as Nan touched her with a leg, Chica threw up her head and sprang forward, catching Nan off balance. She lurched back in the saddle. Chica launched into a canter.

It was not a wild canter, though it was fast. Chica was perfectly in control. But Nan was not doing the controlling.

Elen could swear the mare was laughing. "Just like Brychan," she said. Sara's glance asked a question. She answered: "My pony at home."

Sara nodded and smiled. Nan was obviously determined not to cry for help, but nothing she tried, including sawing the reins, was having the least effect. Her expression as she raced past was set and stiff.

After another circuit of the arena without visible change in speed, Bran stepped calmly out in front of the rocketing mare and said, "That will do, thank you, ma'am."

Chica threw up her head and snorted and danced and skidded to a halt. Nan managed to stick to the saddle, but when she swung her leg over and slid to the ground, she had to stand and just breathe. Sweat ran down her cheeks. Her face was too dark to go pale, but there was a distinctly greyish cast around the lips.

Bran handed her a bottle of water. She took a long drink, then tipped the rest into her palm and splashed her head and neck.

Chica tossed her head and snorted. She had barely broken a sweat.

While Nan wobbled back into the line, baring her teeth at Nick, who was collecting coins from Lucas and Matt, Bran handed Chica's rein to Sara. "Cool her out?" Sara asked, as if she knew the answer but wanted to be careful about assuming anything.

He nodded.

"Hey, no fair!" said Matt. "What kind of test is that?"

"My kind of test," Bran answered.

That barely stopped Matt. "Well, I don't see how it's a test. She's from here. She knows all the horses. *She'll* get into the school no matter what."

Sara rounded on him. "No, I won't."

"Sure you will," said Matt. "You're family. Your parents—"

"*Don't* talk about my parents," Sara said quietly. Matt opened his mouth to keep on braying at her, but met her eyes and went white. Elen heard his teeth click together.

"You're all being tested here," said Bran. "No matter who you are." Did he glance at Elen and Ria when he said that?

Elen told herself she was being foolish. Sara mounted Chica, and Nan groaned, though she laughed, too. For Sara, the mare was a different horse. She was still lively and energetic, but her gaits were no more than normally fast, and she was perfectly obedient to leg and seat and rein.

Matt was right, as far as he went. For Sara this was not really a test, unless Bran was testing something other than her ability to mount and ride basic figures. He must be: Sara rode more carefully than Elen suspected she might normally do, and followed every instruction to the letter.

When she finished, Bran called Ria. The Caledonian had taken refuge in what shade there was, over by the barn, and was looking gratifyingly wilted. She came forward willingly, even so.

Chica whickered at her. The mare had tolerated Nan, apart from delivering a withering commentary on her riding skills, and had clearly known and liked Sara, but this was real tenderness.

It made Elen's gut clench. She would die before she confessed to jealousy, but this was unbearable. How could a horse, any horse, love a Caledonian at first sight?

Ria smoothed the wispy dark mane and murmured something that Elen could not catch, then ran through the check of tack and horse and mounted with calm and unspectacular skill.

No matter how much Elen hated to see it, the girl could ride. Chica tucked her round spotted quarters and arched her delicate neck and showed them all that she could dance.

Even Matt was slack-jawed. Nick let out a long whistle. "Sweet," he said.

Ria did not seem to notice. What attention she spared from her riding was on Bran—and Bran wore no expression at all.

Some people were born to sit on the back of a horse. Elen would have killed for legs as long as Ria's, and a back so straight and yet so supple that it flowed with every stride. If it had been anyone else from any other world, she would have bowed before that grace and that effortless skill.

But it was a Caledonian. That took all the joy out of it.

When Elen's turn finally came, she had sense enough not to throw herself into the saddle, but to take her time as the others had, and ask the mare's permission before she mounted. Chica whickered at her, which would have delighted her to no end if the fickle thing had not done it for Ria first.

Chica was every bit as light and willing as she had seemed. Three riders before Elen had barely quickened her breathing. She fit Elen well: just the right size, just the right rhythm. Elen caught herself breaking out in a smile when Bran called for that smooth and flowing but subtly springy trot, and then the slow sea-roll of the canter.

She stopped caring about riding better than Ria—almost. She wanted to ride well because it made things easier for Chica.

There was no way to hold on to hate or anger while she rode. After she finished she would focus her mind in loathing Ria again. For now, the whole world was the horse under her and the wind in her hair and the sun lifting her up instead of beating her down.

When Bran called for a halt, Elen almost cried out

in protest. She remembered just in time and held her tongue. She dismounted as slowly as she could, lingering to stroke Chica's neck and loosen her girth and make sure she was properly cooled out.

The stablehand, whose name was Francisco, waited patiently for Elen to let go. When she finally could bear to, he met her eyes and smiled.

He understood. So did Bran. The others, Elen realized, were unusually quiet. "Well," said Nick, who usually let the others do the talking, "that's cleared up, then. We're all riders here."

"You are," Bran said. "Whether you're horsemen, too—that needs more time to tell. How are you all at cleaning tack?"

The boys groaned. Lilly shook her head at them. "Lazy gits. Riding's the reward. You earn it cleaning tack and mucking stalls and feeding and grooming."

"I *like* horsework," Ria said before Elen could get the words out. "I like anything that lets me be around horses."

Elen hated to agree with that, and Ria of all people. But it was true. The other girls nodded and murmured assent. Elen settled for striding out ahead of everyone, and being the first in the tack room—which gave her first choice of what to do. She went for the saddles, leaving the bits and bridles to the boys.

The girls all grinned at her—yes, even Ria. They

really were a tribe then, passing bars of saddle soap back and forth and wielding sponges with practiced skill.

After tack cleaning was stall cleaning. They won a pause at midday to eat and rest in the cool of the lodge, then Bran herded them back to it in the heat of the afternoon.

Elen had started to adapt, but from everything she could see, Ria was miserable. Most of Caledon was wet and cold, and parts of it were frozen in ice through the whole of the year. Hot sun and burning deserts were alien to her, and her fair skin burned with terrible speed.

Even after the sun had sunk low enough to send shadows stretching long across the corrals, the heat refused to let up. Bran had them all grooming horses in the barn, where at least there was shade and a line of ceiling fans down the aisleway.

They were working two to a horse. Elen had paired more than happily with Sara. Ria was next up the aisle with Nan, soldiering grimly on though her face was scarlet.

Sara saw Elen watching Ria, turned and looked, and frowned. Suddenly she brightened with the onset of an idea. "Listen, everybody! It's crazy hot. Let's bag the brushes and have a horse wash instead."

If Ria had never existed, Elen would have thought that was a grand idea. The rest leaped on it. Matt even whooped. "First dibs on the shower stall!"

"Sure, you can have it!" Sara called back. "We're going outside to the wash racks."

Ria looked disgustingly grateful for the chance to cool off. Elen dug in her heels. "Bran said groom horses, not wash them. He's got to be still testing us. This whole camp is a test, isn't it? Remember what happened this morning when people didn't do what he said."

Six pairs of eyes stared at her over horses' backs and around horses' necks. Lilly spoke for them all. "Have you gone daft? It's bleedin' hot. Clean horses, cool people—how can you argue with that?"

"I just don't think we're supposed to," Elen said, watching Ria wilt. It was small and mean and unbecoming of her family or her position, but she was glad. She wanted Ria to suffer. She deserved it. Every Caledonian did, no matter who or where she was.

"She's probably right," Ria said. She started off faint, but her voice grew louder as if she had managed to push it out in the open. "We'd better do what we're told. Just for today—just in case."

Elen sucked in a breath of hot dusty air. "Oh, no, you don't! You're not going to get me to change my mind just because you agree with me."

"Of course not," Ria said. "I wouldn't dream of it. Unlike you, *I* want to stay."

"So do I!" Elen flung back at her.

All at once Elen realized there was no horse beside her any longer. Sara had snapped off the crossties and led the big bay gelding toward the far end of the barn. The pinto Ria and Nan had been working on was already halfway there, following the two others that had been assigned to the boys and Lilly. Elen and Ria were all alone in the barn aisle, glaring at each other, while the rest of camp went on without them.

"I'll tell Bran!" Elen yelled at the deserters.

None of them answered. Their silence was a distinct and pointed rebuke. In it, Elen heard the hiss of a hose.

Ria turned her back on Elen and trotted off down the aisle. She would probably have run if there had been enough left of her. Even going that fast made her wheeze: Elen could hear her struggling to breathe.

"Oh, stop it," Elen said. "You'll die and they'll all blame me. All I want you to do is suffer."

Ria halted and spun. She almost fell over; she caught herself against a stall door. "Isn't that just like an Ymbrian? Petty and mean and always ready to throw the blame on someone else."

"No," said Elen, viciously precise. "That's Caledon. Go play with the hoses, winter girl. You'll never survive your time here if you don't learn to cool off."

"I won't survive at all if you have anything to say about it."

"You said it," said Elen. "I didn't."

Ria snarled at her, spun back around and stalked off toward the wash racks. Elen almost refused to follow. But everyone else was there, and cold water on heat-tormented skin was the best thing in the world.

CHAPTER 7

That evening, when they were all done to a turn and ready to collapse into their cool beds, Megan and Bran freed them for a brief rest and shower and change of clothes. Dinner on the first full night of camp was special: a sort of feast called a barbecue.

The heat went down somewhat at last with the sun, and the clouds that had built up above the mountains melted into the clear and burning sky. Bran and some of the hands lit a fire in the pit behind the barn. The air was full of the sweet and pungent smell of ribs and chicken grilling over mesquite wood.

There was corn, too, roasted in the husk, and pots of beans tasting of sharp-sweet sauce and smoke, and tubs full of wonderful things that the rest of the tribe were happy to name for Elen: coleslaw and potato salad, chips and salsa and guacamole, and a vat of green salad that she could have gone swimming in. There were metal cans of cold and oddly prickly drinks called soda, and water and juice and a tall urn of hot bitter coffee and another of ice-cold tea.

It was a feast worthy of kings. Elen hardly knew where to begin. She filled a plate with a little of everything, let Nick pour her a glass of tea, and retreated through the small crowd of ranch hands and campers to the table nearest the barn. The rest of the tribe settled there with her, watching the shadows of horses in the dusk and the rising moonlight. Conversation was light, easy: people talked about where they came from around about Earth, and how they had come to the House of the Star.

"We live in Australia," Nan said, "on a pimple in the Outback called Jack's Crossing. We've a mob of horses and cattle and sheep, and our mum raises pigs."

"And you came all the way out here to spend the summer on another ranch?" Sara asked.

Nan laughed. "We did. We're all mad out there in Oz, didn't you know?"

"It gets her out of school," Matt pointed out. He

grinned at Nan. "You people are all backwards, having winter when it's summer."

"From where I sit," said Lilly, "*you're* the backwards ones. You ride your horses upside down, your water swirls the wrong way, and when you dig a hole, you end up in China."

"Where do *you* end up?" Sara wanted to know.

"Why," said Lilly, "here!"

The boys hooted. Elen smiled in the dusk and the light of torches—until she glanced toward the end of the table. Then her smile died.

Ria hovered there, perched on the bench as if she meant to take flight at any moment. She picked at the food on her plate but seemed uninterested in it.

Too much sun could do that. Lilly, next to Ria, made her drink a whole bottle of water and start another. "You've got to keep the water coming," she said. "This is desert. It will dry you up and blow you away before you know you're even thirsty."

Whatever Ria answered, Elen was too far away to hear. Lucas and Matt had got up a contest to see who could eat the most ribs the fastest. It was noisy as well as sticky.

Elen ducked flying ribs and worked her way around her plate, savoring each strange or half-familiar thing. After all she had done to avoid being here, and even after the shock of discovering Caledon's latest outrage against both Earth and Ymbria, Elen realized she was happy. It was surprising and a little humiliating. But the humiliation did not last very long.

There was only one thing lacking. None of the horses now invisible in the dark was Blanca. Even lovely spotted Chica was not the same.

Elen missed Blanca. It struck her in a wave as strong as homesickness, with a memory of large white warmth and spreading calm.

She would never have expected to feel such a thing. The mare had forced her to come here and made sure she stayed. Elen should resent her bitterly.

Blanca was far above resentment. She simply was. Elen had a powerful urge to be close to her. It was so strong she almost stood up and ran off in the direction it was calling her to, but some faint remnant of sense kept her where she was.

The rules were just as clear as Blanca's call. Campers stayed here, where the horses were mortal and the camp was entirely of Earth. The other part of the ranch, the part where the worldrunners were, was not for them. Not until they had finished with camp and been chosen for the worldriders' school.

The barbecue ended with a bonfire and a round of singing. The songs were Earth songs, but Elen had a quick ear. Some she was glad to learn. Others, like the interminable one about beer, she hoped she would never have to suffer through again.

When the fire shrank to embers and the songs

faded to a drowsy murmur, Megan and Bran rounded up the campers and herded them to the cabins. Even Matt and Lucas went obediently, stumbling with sleepiness.

Elen's body was out on its feet, but her mind was wide awake. She lay in the bunk, listening to the others' breathing. Sara slept neat and quiet. Ria tossed and fretted in her sleep, and when she flung herself onto her back, she snored.

The longer Elen lay there, the faster her mind ran. It was full of Blanca: the sight and smell of her, the smooth power of her stride, and the depth and width of her body when Elen sat on her.

She must be out on the worldroads again tonight, carrying a rider on some errand of terrible importance. Elen was simply yesterday's parcel, delivered and now forgotten.

Elen could not bear to believe that. Blanca must remember her. Horses remembered everything.

She needed Blanca to remember. That need was stronger than any rule or law.

She slipped out of bed. Neither of the others moved. She pulled jeans on under her sleeping shirt, and put on her own shoes from Ymbria rather than the stiff new ones from Earth.

The door latch's click seemed terribly loud, but no challenge rang out. Elen eased it open, slid through, then ever so carefully eased it shut.

The night air was soft and warm and full of strange, dry scents. Far off in the hills, something yip-yip-yipped. Elen lifted her face to the stars.

There were so many. Ymbria's stars poured in streams down the night sky, with deep and formless darkness between. Here they were everywhere, scattered from horizon to horizon.

She had to look down before she fell into them. She kept her eyes fixed on the ground as she picked her way across the sandy square.

The glimmer of starlight caught the outline of a gate in the wall, opening directly opposite to the Earthly half of the ranch. That gate was not visible in daylight. When the sun shone, that part of the wall seemed blank and unbroken.

Elen knew all the way down to her bones what was on the other side of the gate. Worldrunners. Blanca.

Blanca *did* remember. She was waiting. Elen could feel her. She wanted Elen to go where she was.

"I'll get expelled," Elen said to her. "Then I'll never see you again."

No, Blanca said. *Come.*

The bolt slid easily. Elen's heart was beating hard, drumming in her ears.

The air as she passed through the gate had an odd

feel to it, tingling on her skin. She stopped, struck with fear, but the path ahead of her had no sense about it of a worldroad. She was still on Earth, and still on the ranch.

The barn was still there, too, looming in the starlight. Windows in the upper story were mostly dark, but a handful were lit, most along the far end.

Riders lived there. She knew as much about them as anyone not a rider could: how they studied for years on this and other ranches on Earth, and when at last they were accepted to ride the worldroads, they lived above their horses, sharing space with one another and eating in common.

It was a stark life, focused intensely on their duty. It was dangerous—deadly, even, as they rode in ones and twos along the worldroads, carrying messages and guiding travelers and keeping order among the worlds.

Elen hid in the darkness, watching to see if anyone came out. Everything was quiet. Even the wind was still, and the creatures of the night had gone silent.

Somewhere in the barn, a horse snorted. Elen should turn around and go back to the cabin and be a good and obedient camper. But Blanca was there, waiting for her to find the courage to go in.

Elen glided toward the bulk of the barn. It smelled of dust and heat and horses. The big doors at the ends were too heavy and loud to move without waking half the ranch, but a small one far down the side opened for her.

There were protections here. They were buried deep and all but invisible, but they had held for years out of count.

They let Elen in, because she had Blanca's call inside her. She walked down the aisle. It was dim-lit at either end, nearly dark in the middle.

Blanca was in the last stall on the right, with her name on the door. She lifted her head and whickered at Elen.

That sweet soft sound drew her in. She wrapped her arms around the warm silken neck. She would have slept standing there if she could. She almost did, there in the warm dimness.

The barn exploded into light. Elen clamped herself against Blanca. The mare stood perfectly steady.

Voices echoed down the aisle. Hooves clattered. One set clip-clopped as it should; the other moved slowly, hesitantly. That one was lame or hurt.

Elen's heart stopped trying to leap out of her chest. She hardly knew what she would do if she was caught, but she had to see. Cautiously she peered above the stall door.

Two worldriders led horses down the aisle, with others ahead and behind. John David was there. So, Elen saw with a faint shock, was Bran.

The riders were covered with dust and ash; the

edges of their coats were singed. The black gelding who walked sound looked as if he had lost part of his tail.

The bay mare behind him made Elen catch her breath and swallow a soft cry. Her whole side and flank were terribly burned; her right fore glistened with blood and worse: the white gleam of bone.

The stall across from Blanca's was different from the others. There was no soft bedding in it; its floor was thickly padded, and it was almost painfully clean. A woman waited there with a cart full of bandages and salves and other things that Elen did not know enough to recognize, and a machine that hummed softly to itself.

Bran led the mare into the stall. The poor thing was nearly out on her feet; she staggered over the threshold but managed not to fall.

While Bran and the woman set to work on her, the rider with the black gelding led him into a stall down the aisle. John David stayed outside the mare's stall with her charred and visibly shaken rider.

"It's getting worse," the rider said. "We couldn't get to Hybrazeal at all. There are fissures in the road past Morganach, and the firedrakes had broken through. One of them found us before we could get the wards back up. I tried to get Kellen to go on while I brought Miri back, but he wouldn't."

"Of course I wouldn't," Kellen said from the gelding's stall. He sounded exhausted, but there was a distinct edge to his tone. "You know that's not how we work."

"Sometimes rules are for breaking," the rider said. Her anger was fiercer than his, but then she shook her head and sighed, and the faint crackle of lightning died away. "No matter. It's done. That part of the road is repairable, now we've been warned, but what about the rest? I don't know that we can wait for your experiment to succeed. If you're thinking they'll start to warm up after six weeks, both get into the school, and then manage not to kill each other for the years it takes to become a rider, that's all very well. But the worldroads are breaking up *now*. They'll be lucky to last another month."

"We'll have to do what we can," John David said. He sounded tired, too, but there was steel under it. "As long as Caledon and Ymbria stand under forced truce, at least they can't make things worse."

"You don't think they'll try?" the rider said. She shed her coat and hat and raked fingers through short-cropped, greying brown hair. "I don't trust a one of them, and that includes the young pups they sent to snap at each other on our watch."

"Trust has to begin somewhere," John David said. "I'll send down food and drink and a cot, and one of the medics to see to those burns."

"I'm all right," she said brusquely. "Hungry and thirsty, that's all."

"I'm sure," said John David with a glance that made clear what he really thought. He gripped her shoulder briefly, nodded and left her.

It looked as if the worldrider was going to camp in front of Blanca's stall. Elen looked around desperately. The back of the stall had a latch on it: instead of two metal panels bolted together as she had thought, one slid aside, opening onto a small, pipe-fenced corral.

It was wrenchingly hard to leave Blanca in the stall and escape into the night. But the last thing Elen needed was for the worldriders to find her and accuse her of spying.

She was in shock. She had never cared what others thought of Ymbria. It was her world; it deserved to survive in any way it could.

She had not expected that people would hate it. Everybody hated the long war, and of course they hated Caledon. But Ymbria was different.

The worldriders did not think so. Both worlds had taken their war everywhere it could be taken, and done damage from one end of the worldroad to the other. Ymbria was just as much at fault for that as Caledon.

They must blame Elen for what they thought her people had done, just as much as they blamed Ria for hers. That hurt in ways Elen could barely begin to describe.

She ran through a blur of tears and rising rage, with just enough sense left not to blunder into the worldriders' sight. The faster she ran, the harder it was to stop. The only thing that did bring her up short, in the end, was the cabin's door, with Sara and Ria still sound asleep inside. Neither would ever know that she had been gone, or where, or what she had seen and heard.

She made a vow of that, as she lay in her unfamiliar bed. She would keep it secret inside her. She would never tell.

CHAPTER 8

In those first days at the ranch, Elen learned to live on the Earth that knew nothing of worldrunners or worldroads, and had never heard of Ymbria or Caledon or the long war. There were guests in cabins out past the house and the barns, and those were as mortal as anyone could be. Most of the horses in the barns were there for them. In winter, camp was for them, too. Meanwhile campers were not to speak of any but Earthly things, and if they met the other guests, it was best if they said nothing at all.

It was very strange, and it kept Elen from thinking

too much about what she had seen and heard in that other barn. She ran with the tribe, spending her days in the barns and her evenings in the cool of the lodge, learning the lore of Earth as well as the rest of the worlds.

She decided, after she came back through the hidden gate, to ignore Ria instead of fighting with her. Everyone expected them to fight. Even worldriders who had never met either of them were talking about it.

If there was anything Elen hated as much as she hated Caledon, it was being predictable. She made up her mind to do the opposite of what they all thought she would do. She pretended Ria did not exist. She stayed as far away from the zone of nonexistence as she could. She never spoke to it or about it. Even in the cabin at night, she did her best to act as if it had never been there at all.

She could have spun that out forever, if she had been able to stop thinking of Blanca. No matter which horse she rode in the daylight, when she closed her eyes, it was that long white face she saw, and that dark deep stare.

Blanca had got under her skin. She could no more resist it than she could resist the urge to breathe.

Five days into camp, Elen's campaign of rendering Ria nonexistent was succeeding magnificently, in her estimation. That day, instead of looking after the guest horses, the campers had a new assignment: to clean stalls in the breeding barn.

These horses were not worldrunners. They were working cow horses: a common breed and type in this part of Earth, and Rancho Estrella was known for producing fine stock. That morning Bran introduced them all to the stallions. The massively muscled chestnut was named King; he was a Quarter Horse. Dreamer was the same breed as Chica, an Appaloosa; he was white all over, with striking black spots, some of which were as big as Elen's hand.

Bran put Elen and Sara in charge of cleaning the stud barn while he led the rest of the campers away to clean up after the mares. "Some people have all the luck," Matt said.

"Some people didn't try to get out of cleaning stalls yesterday by dumping a load of shavings over the old manure," Sara reminded him.

"That wasn't us!" Lilly protested.

"No, and you won't be mucking out the mares, either," Bran said. "That's the boys' job. You and Nan and Ria, you're on shavings patrol. Sara and Elen, when you're done with the stallions, go back there and help them."

The boys' objections were loud and long, and no

one paid the least attention. Mucking was the nasty part. Shavings patrol was easy: fill the big red cart with sweet-smelling wood shavings, haul its wonderfully light weight down to each stall, and spread the contents over the newly cleaned floor.

The stud barn was hardly any trouble to clean. Francisco led King and Dreamer out to big oblong pens under the mesquite trees. Elen and Sara each took one of the empty stalls and went to work.

Elen was faster with the muck fork than Sara. "Where'd you learn to clean that fast?" Sara demanded as Elen rattled past her with the manure cart. "I thought you were a royal princess."

"I was," Elen said, halting. "I am. I grew up cleaning stalls. My mother believes that children should pick up after themselves."

"You didn't have any servants?"

"We had hundreds. We still did our own chores."

Sara shook her head. "Amazing."

Elen grinned. As she moved on past the stall Sara was cleaning, she glanced into the next one down, and her grin faded. That one needed cleaning, too, and the piles in it were no older than those in the stall Elen had just finished.

She sighed, but Sara was still picking her slow way through King's stall, and this was not so very bad. "Sara!" she called as she set to work. "Who's the third stallion?"

"Who?" Sara called back. "Oh. They must have decided to use Moondance after all. I thought Uncle John said—"

She broke off and did not go on, even when Elen asked, "Uncle John what?"

Elen thought about pushing for an answer, but she was nearly done and she could always ask later. She pitched the last pile into the nearly full cart, raked through the shavings that were left, and found them dry and still sweet. "That will do," she said.

The manure spreader waited outside the stud barn, not far from the stallions' pens. While Elen emptied the cart into it, she peered down along the line of pens. Red King was closest, then spectacularly spotted Dreamer. There was someone else in the pen past that.

Elen wandered on down. Sara was still slogging through her one stall. Everybody else was hard at work cleaning up after the mares. There was no one to stop Elen from meeting Moondance.

Moondance was young and awkward and full of himself. He looked like nothing in particular: a small, roundish, greyish, blocky creature with a head too big for the rest of him. But that would change when he was older. He was like Blanca. He was a worldrunner.

Elen leaned on the bars of his pen. He was eating hay from a tire feeder in a corner, keeping an ear trained on her but not interested enough to abandon his breakfast and investigate.

"Well," she said. "Aren't you a surprise. What are you doing here instead of being locked up safe with the rest of your people?"

He might be a worldrunner, but he was nothing like Blanca. He made no effort to communicate with Elen. He ate his breakfast and snorted at his rivals and acted in all ways like a normal and ordinary horse.

It was a little disappointing. Elen sighed and ambled back to the manure cart. She still had to stow it and move on to the shavings bin. Sara had finally finished: she was on her way to the spreader.

A flicker of movement caught Elen's eye. Someone had slipped out of the mares' barn and angled down toward the mesquite grove.

It was Ria. Elen opened her mouth to let Bran know the Caledonian had sneaked away from her work again. But that would mean acknowledging the Caledonian's existence.

Someone else could get her in trouble today. She was always slipping away: the heat was no easier on her now than it had been on the first day, and her milk-white skin hated the sun. This time she stood in the shade of the trees, watching Moondance with a look of hunger on her face.

She was mad for horses, like the rest of the tribe. But just now she seemed madder than usual.

That was odd enough to keep Elen from turning

away and letting herself forget Ria existed. Ria moved slowly down the line of the fence. She hesitated when she came near the edge of the shade, then pressed on as if she could not help herself.

Moondance was not ignoring Ria at all, not the way he had ignored Elen. He watched closely, quiet but alert, the way stallions do. Ria made her way to the corner and stopped. Elen thought she might slip through the fence, but she held still.

Moondance shook his mane and snorted. Ria stood motionless. He cantered down off the hill, straight toward her.

She seemed frozen in place. The stallion stretched his neck impossibly, arching it over the fence.

His nose was directly in Ria's face. His breath ruffled her hair. Ria raised her hand to stroke the big grey-white head, rubbing under the chin and up toward the little curling ears. Moondance sighed and rested his forehead against her chest.

He only did it for the space of a breath. They both let go at once. Ria stumbled back. Moondance spun and bolted up the hill.

Ria turned and ran.

Elen almost did the same. She caught herself up against the manure cart. *So that's what it looks like from the outside,* she thought.

Maybe Moondance had done the same thing to Ria that Blanca had done to Elen. Could a person love a horse so much but be so afraid of what she felt that she hardly made sense to herself?

Those were not comfortable thoughts, because Elen understood them. She did not want to understand the Caledonian. But Blanca did the same to her.

At least she did not run like a coward when it happened.

That afternoon in the lodge, instead of Megan, John David came to teach them. That put them all on their best behavior, even the boys.

Those late-afternoon classes were the only time they ever talked about anything but Earth and mortal horses. For an hour before dinner, they were allowed to remember what they were really doing here and what they hoped to become.

The past few days they had been studying about worldroads, or as Megan called them, straight tracks: where they went, and why one should only step off them if there was no other possible choice.

Elen listened to be polite, but not because she expected to learn anything new. John David had come to tell them an old story, one of the oldest of all, about how the people of Earth discovered that some horses could always follow a straight track, and always go where their riders wanted to go.

"Always?" Matt said. "You're talking about horses here. Horses are the twistiest travelers I ever met."

"I said *some* horses," John David said. "That was the miracle: to discover which ones were born to travel straight."

Someone was supposed to ask. It was a game; Elen was in a mood to play. "How did they discover that?"

"Well now," said John David, "there's a story. It was a bard in Wales, many hundred years ago, who made such a song for a clan chieftain that the chieftain offered him anything he wanted that the clan had to offer. He chose a sturdy grey horse—pony we'd say now—whose dam had been a mountain pony but whose sire was a Roman commander's charger. Romans as a nation were not the greatest horsemen, but this one came from Sarmatia where everyone was born in the saddle, and his silver-grey stallion was the finest that anyone in Wales had seen.

"The stallion's daughter took after her dam, being stocky and sensible, though she was a little bigger, and she had her father's moonlight coat. She'd been a great disappointment; the chieftain had hoped for a glorious charger of his own, and got just another pony.

"But the bard looked in the young mare's eye, and what he saw there made him realize that this was a horse like no other. The chieftain was glad to give her up and the bard was glad to take her, and off he rode down the track in the morning. When he came to the end of it, he'd ridden right out of the world."

"He must have wanted to do that," Ria said, "because you said—"

"Oh, yes," John David said, "he was looking for a new patron, and he'd taken it into his head that the king of the Otherworld might pay better for songs than the kings and chieftains of Wales. The bard was a little touched in the head, people said, and I wouldn't argue with that. He'd heard all the warnings: that the folk on the other side were strange and wild and in no way human, even the ones that looked it; and a man who stepped across the threshold might stay for a day and find he'd been gone a hundred years. But the bard had no fear of ending up in the future: he wasn't enthralled with the present that he lived in.

"So he rode out of an Earthly hill fort and into the courts of Annwn, and the horse who carried him was as calm about it as if she did it every day."

"Maybe she did," Nick said.

"Maybe," said John David. "She was the first worldrunner that Earth ever knew, and it turned out her foals had the same gift. As for the bard, he spent a year in Annwn, making songs for its lords and ladies, and sometimes for the lord of the dread Hunt. They say he even rode the skies one wild night, making order in the lands of Faerie and reaping a harvest of souls. But that's only hearsay, because he never would speak of it, nor would he turn it into a song.

"After a year had passed, the bard went exploring. He found other worlds to which his mare also knew the way—including two that weren't enemies yet, though they would be later. When he came back to Earth, he'd been gone ten years, and ten years had passed here, too; so that story was proved false. Though there had been times when it was true, and would be again."

"What times?" Elen asked for them all. "What happened then?"

"All sorts of things," John David said.

"Tell us about the long war," Matt said before Elen could ask her next question. "Was the bard there when it started? Did he have anything to do with it?"

"I think," said John David, "that that is a story for another day."

Matt might have pushed, but Elen's glare stopped him. So did Ria's. When he backed down, they found themselves face to face, glare to glare—agreeing on something.

As soon as Elen realized what she was doing, she flicked her glance away. She could feel Ria doing the same. That was maddening, too, but not as much as what had come before.

There was an hour yet until dinner. The heat outside was as fierce as it had been since Elen came to Earth; it had physical weight, bearing down on a body until it lay gasping in the dust.

Clouds piled up on the mountains, teasing but never quite keeping their promise. That was how it was in this season, everybody said. The heat rose and rose and rose, until finally it broke in a crash of thunder and a blaze of lightning. Then the rains came, pounding the parched earth, turning dry washes to rivers and waking the dead land.

It was cool in the lodge. Even the boys were quiet, bent over their books. Ria was off by herself again.

She was doing that more and more. At first Lilly or Nan or Sara had tried to lure her into the middle with the rest of the tribe, but Ria insisted that she liked to curl up with her back to the wall. That was warrior thinking: as if anyone here, even Elen, could be that kind of threat to her.

She had a book in her lap and her head was bent over it, but Elen had not seen her turn a page. She might be asleep, or she might be doing what Caledonians did better than anything else: plotting treachery.

Maybe she was homesick. Elen would rather not have been that close to sympathy, but she had to be fair. That was the tribe infecting her, and the ranch and the horses. Fairness mattered a great deal to a horse.

A horse could hate another of its kind just as ferociously as a human could. Elen crushed down any desire to ask Ria what the trouble was, and turned her back on her, facing inward toward the rest of the tribe.

CHAPTER 9

Earth measured time in a confusing number of ways, but Elen understood the week almost at once. That was five days of work and rest, and then two days of more work and less rest called the weekend.

The first weekend of camp, the tribe underwent a test of sorts: riders came from outside, from the Earth that knew nothing of worldroads, for something called team penning. That involved horses, cattle, and a great deal of running and herding.

It began late in the searingly hot day, when the mountains' shadows stretched long across the valley, and lasted until after dark. Some of the hands thought that the clouds heaped up above the mountains would finally let go their burden of rain, but they only tempted and teased and flirted with lightning.

The strangers rolled in in their metal cars, unloaded their horses and staked out territory outside the arena. Inside, a small herd of calves milled in a pen.

The rest of the tribe were terribly excited. They all knew what this thing was. The boys claimed to have won championships at home. Lilly and Nan were less full of nonsense, but they prodded Sara into admitting that she was rather good at it.

"Rather!" Nan mocked her. "You won the winter championship, and got a whacking big belt buckle for it, too."

Sara flushed and mumbled. "It wasn't just me. It was the team."

"Which you led," said Nan. "We're claiming you this time. Don't say no."

Sara glanced at Elen and Ria. "I don't know—"

"Go," said Elen. "I want to watch before I try it."

Ria had nothing to add to that, even if Elen had cared. Sara wavered a little longer, but between Elen's firm stare and Nan's tugging hand, she gave in.

Chasing cattle, even on horseback, was not a thing a princess did in Ymbria. Even so, Elen had to admit it looked interesting.

It seemed simple enough, though that did not mean it was easy. Three riders had to pen three cattle out of the herd. The cattle were numbered; the riders had to find, herd, and pen only those with the number that was called out when they crossed the starting line—and do it faster than any other team, and without letting the rest of the herd into the pen.

It was wonderfully confusing, with much thundering of hooves and yelling of riders and lowing of cattle. The strangers from elsewhere were good and they were fast. Rancho Estrella's boys might have been faster, if Lucas had not forgotten he was riding Max and tried to kick him into an extra burst of speed. Lucas ended up flat on his back inside the pen, and the calf he had been chasing escaped and ran back to its herd. That was the end of it for the boys—and left Sara and the twins to defend the honor of the ranch.

Sara forgot to be humble once she was mounted on her favorite horse, a cranky little sorrel named Cheddar. Lilly and Nan took positions behind her at the starting line. Their horses waited with varying degrees of impatience for the announcer's voice to roar out the number: *Six!*

They darted toward the knot of cattle. Sara led, aiming straight for a red-spotted calf with a bright blue number 6 painted on his rump. Lilly chose a black calf and Nan a white-faced red. The twins' calves were as obedient as cattle ever were, but Sara's had a temper and a talent for hiding behind a handful of its larger and differently numbered brothers.

Sara pointed Cheddar at a vanishingly narrow gap in the herd. Cheddar pinned her ears back and snaked her head and snapped at a dusty white calf that veered across her path. The calf ducked away. Their quarry bounced off a big black calf and dived for the fence, but Cheddar caught him on the bounce and shouldered him straight into the pen with the other two calves. Sara's hand was just about to fly up and signal victory when the black calf bulled past her into the pen.

"Four calves in the pen!" the announcer bellowed. "Team number five disqualified!"

Elen groaned as loudly as anyone else. The team tried to put a good face on it, but Sara looked ready to cry. Even Cheddar seemed to feel the sting of the defeat: he left the arena with his head down and his ears flat.

"Here," Bran said behind her. "Mount up and get ready. We're up after the next two teams."

She spun. Bran stood with Chica and his own leopard-spotted Orgoch. Ria was already mounted beyond, on a pretty and very fast little black bay named Sharif.

"I can't do this," Elen said. "I've never even—"

"You can ride," he said. "Chica knows how to pen. Stay out of her way and let her do her job."

He held out the reins. Chica's neat little ears were pricked, watching Elen. Her nostrils fluttered ever so slightly.

"Is this a bribe?" Elen asked both of them.

"Yes," said Bran. "Come on. There's just enough time to limber up before we have to go."

It was more than a bribe, Elen thought. She had to ride in a team with Ria—that was deliberate and calculated. So, she suspected bitterly, was Sara's failure with the calves.

Sara would not do that. Would she?

Who knew what anyone would do? Elen snatched the reins and sprang onto Chica's back without touching the stirrups—showing off and knowing it, and not caring if anybody hated her for it.

Chica shook her ears at the heat of Elen's temper, but otherwise ignored it. The two teams penned their calves and withdrew, with neither having managed to match the fastest time.

The team that meant to win was lounging at the rail, three wild-haired girls in identically tattered jeans. They had beaten all the boys handily, and left the girls in the dust.

One of them caught Elen staring at her and grinned. It was a perfectly friendly grin, and made it perfectly clear that she knew who was going to take the prize.

Elen did not even know what the prize was. At that particular moment, she did not care at all. She was going to win it.

She and Bran would win it, and if Ria kept out of

the way, well and good. Elen smoothed the mane on Chica's neck and bent to inhale her warm horse smell. "Show me what to do," she said in the waiting ear.

It was almost time. Elen settled deeper in the saddle and wiped sweat from her forehead with her sleeve. The sun had gone down without her noticing it; the lights were glaring bright. The heat was less, and that was good, but it was still strong.

When she looked up, lightning traced the jagged line of the mountaintops. She almost missed the starter's signal, but Chica was ready. "Number nine!" the announcer sang.

Chica aimed straight into the herd. The arena was big enough and the herd spread out enough that Elen found it easier than she had feared to spot the three calves with the blue 9 on their rumps.

Bran pointed toward the cream-colored one, and headed for it. There was still a white-faced black one and one that was solid black.

Elen's glance crossed Ria's. In the instant before they remembered to clash, they knew exactly what to do. Ria would take the black—it was closer to her. That left the white-faced one.

Sharif threw up his head and tail and bounced toward the black calf. Chica had less silliness in her. She tucked her hindquarters, gathered herself, and set to work.

The calf darted and ducked and tried to hide.

Wherever he was, Chica was there before him. Before either the calf or Elen knew what had happened, he was running beside the black calf toward the pen, and Sharif and Chica were neck and neck. Ria's knee almost brushed Elen's. They traded wild grins as the calves dived into the pen with Bran's pale calf bawling behind them.

Bran's arm swung up. The announcer called the time. "Forty-six seconds!"

Elen whooped. Ria shrilled a war cry. Forty-seven had been the time to beat, and they had beaten it.

Winning felt wonderful. The prize turned out to be a bronze medallion on a blue ribbon, with a star on one side and a mountain on the other. Elen recognized the tall pointed shape of the peak that stood directly over the ranch: when she looked up, she could see it outlined in lightning.

She wore the medallion to the barbecue afterward, as much because it was pretty as because she was proud of it. The wild girls had red ribbons without medallions; they made headbands of theirs, and came to congratulate Ria and Elen and Bran.

They had their eyes on Bran, but he belonged to the tribe and he knew it. He sat with them at their table and shared a platter of ribs.

Elen was hungry enough to eat a whole side of a cow all by herself. She was still full of the victory, and of Chica, who was absolutely wonderful.

Some of the boys from elsewhere came over with offerings: cups of soda or lemonade, and enough chocolate cake to feed the whole table. The boy who brought that was even prettier than Bran. He could have been Ymbrian, with his dark eyes and his lovely manners, bold but shy.

Boys like that had courted Elen at home. She fell easily into the old habit: smiling, trading glances, letting him compliment her.

Ria had slipped out of sight somewhere between putting the horses away and claiming the table for dinner. She must have had to go lie down and recover from the heat.

Elen was glad. It was one thing in the midst of the game to remember how well they might have got on if they had been anything else but what they were. It was another to keep remembering it once the game was over. Ria out of sight was Ria out of mind—and Elen's happiness could be perfect.

CHAPTER 10

After dinner some of the strangers from Earth set themselves up on a platform and began a round of music. It was music meant to dance to, and Elen's courtiers insisted on taking turns. She steered them off toward Sara and Lilly and Nan as much as she could, but the dark-eyed boy was persistent. He kept speaking to her in another language than English, and looking as if he expected her to understand.

"He thinks you're from Spain," Sara explained, "and that's why you won't admit to understanding his Mexican Spanish."

"Spain?" Elen asked. "Why would he think that?"

"Your accent sounds kind of like a Spanish accent," Sara said, "and you look Spanish. Mostly. Really old, really different Spanish—Moorish. I don't suppose you know Arabic? That would put him off the scent for sure."

"I only know your English," Elen said, "and that, it seems, not as well as I thought."

She must have sounded more offended than she felt. Sara looked briefly stricken. "Oh! I'm sorry. I didn't mean—"

"Neither did I," Elen said. She smiled to soothe any sting that might be left, but then she looked past Sara and sighed vastly. "Oh, gods. He's coming back. I don't suppose I could swear at him in Ymbrian?"

"Better not," Sara said with some regret. "Quick, look innocent. I'll try to head him off."

Elen could do better than that: she could welcome a rescue. That one was persistent, too, but he did it in English. He held out his hand and smiled a little tentatively. "Dance?" he said.

"I would be delighted," said Elen.

His whole face lit up. His hand wrapped around hers was damp but not unpleasant, and he let go when they reached the middle of the dance floor. He was tall and lanky and fair-haired, with very long arms and legs. He had grace on a horse—she had noticed him during the penning—but on the ground he went off in all directions.

One of those directions, a few dances in, was to trip Matt as he edged past with a cup of juice in each hand, and send the cups flying straight into Elen's face. It was the alarmingly bright red juice that tasted like nothing but sweet, and it dyed her white shirt crimson.

Poor Josh was mortified. "Oh, God, I'm sorry! I didn't mean to—I had no idea I was going to—"

Matt was just as mortified, for a change, and just as inclined to babble. "Sorry, sorry, I wasn't looking, I should have been more careful, I didn't mean—"

They sounded like a pair of chickens, squawking and clucking and fluttering. Elen was sorely tempted to laugh, and then to knock their heads together.

Josh had the sense to find a cloth and a bowl of water to wash the worst of it, but Elen was still sticky from neck to knees. "I'll go back to the cabin and change," she said.

Every boy within earshot leaped to offer escort. Elen found a smile somewhere and put it on. "Thank you all very much. I'm terribly flattered. But I really would rather take care of it myself."

"But it's dark out," said the too-persistent Hector, who had escaped from Sara's clutches and come racing to her aid. "Who knows what might be lurking on the paths?"

Elen stopped him before he wandered off again down a stream of Spanish. "Nothing will be lurking. It's perfectly safe."

"Coyotes," he said. "Bobcats. Maybe a mountain lion. There was one just last week, down in Sabino; it chased a hiker and nearly—"

Elen had had enough of all this: the night, the music, the crowding strangers. She was tired inside and out. She managed, she hoped, to be polite, but she was blunter than she might have been. "Please. I don't need your help. It's been a pleasure, but I am very sticky and I need to change my shirt."

Their chorus of disappointment made her even more tired. She made one last effort and pushed them toward the rest of the tribe. "Go on. There are my friends. They'll be delighted to share a dance."

Sara, bless her, called to Hector—in Spanish, no less. Elen had to hope it was polite and proper Spanish. Lilly and Nan swooped in and carried off the other two.

Elen was finally, blessedly free. The night was still, not a breath of wind stirring. Past the circle of lights and music and voices and laughter, there was no sound but the distant call of an owl. Even the coyotes were quiet.

She would be glad to wash off the stickiness and the thick, sweet smell, but once she had reassured herself that her medallion and its ribbon had miraculously escaped the flood, she tucked them into a back pocket of her jeans and walked slowly to the cabin.

The dark and the quiet and the peace seeped through her. In the heart of it she found a calm white presence.

Blanca had let Elen be while she settled into the life of the camp. But she was always there, deep down. Sometimes she visited Elen in dreams: coming to ruffle her hair with warm sweet breath, or to carry her on roads of moonlight and starlight, galloping across the sky from dusk until morning.

The square of cabins and lodge and ranch house was dark except for the light above the door of the lodge. Elen's eyes had adjusted to starlight; she could see well enough to walk steadily across the square.

Halfway across, as she passed the ramada, something—a tingle in the spine; a tightening between the shoulders—made her stop. Then she heard the voice.

"I don't think we should do this."

It was Ria. Elen went perfectly still. The ramada was dim inside, but not completely dark. There was light in the middle, faint and pale.

As Elen's eyes adjusted to it, she saw Ria kneeling by the fountain, bent over its basin. It was obvious what she was doing. She was scrying—using the water as a mirror to see far away.

Most scrying was all seeing and no hearing, but Ria was talking, and in the pauses it was clear she was listening. That was a strong spell if she was talking to her people worlds away in Caledon. But then, she had said her mother was a far-seer. Maybe she had the talent, too.

"Yes," she said. "I understand. We are desperate. But this is mad. No one will ever forgive us if we do it."

There was a pause. Elen could gauge how hotly the people on the other end were arguing by how tight Ria's shoulders were. She kept shaking her head and starting to speak, but then stopping as if cut off.

Finally she managed to get a word in. "You don't understand. I can't."

Elen actually heard the dim and distant voice, it called so strongly across the worlds: "*Why* can't you?"

"You don't understand," Ria repeated. "There's no way you can understand without being here. Please just trust me. I can make it work the other way."

The water roared at her. She struck it with her fist, shattering the spell—and very nearly herself.

It rocked Elen all the way outside, and gave her such a headache that she was almost blind with it.

She gathered herself to go in, to see if Ria was still alive—but then she heard that detestably familiar voice, thick with something that might be tears. "I can't. I . . . just . . . can't."

That shook Elen back into herself. Ria was plotting something with her people, just as Elen had always expected that she would, and from the sound of it it was a very bad something. Everything in Elen cried out to her to burst into the ramada, fling the Caledonian's treachery in her face, then haul her off to John David and show him just how hopeless his whole experiment was.

But would he listen? Ria was Caledonian. She would lie. Elen needed proof—something so clear and so obvious that even the Master of the Star would admit that maybe he had been wrong.

Ria had stopped blubbering. She was coming out. Elen shrank as far back into the shadows as she could, and held her breath.

Ria stumbled on past. Elen heard the catch of a sob. Ria probably could not even see where she was going, let alone who was watching her.

Even so, Elen waited for a long count of heartbeats, in case it was a trap and Ria came back to spring it— and probably accuse Elen of being the traitor, too. But Ria was gone.

The ramada was empty and completely silent, and there was no light in it at all. The fountain trickled blindly into its basin. Whatever it had been for Ria, for Elen it was only water. The vision was gone. Elen had no power to bring it back again.

She did try. She even tried to get Blanca to help her, but Blanca had gone down so deep she was hardly there at all. All Elen got for her pains was a worse headache and a heaving stomach.

She managed to keep it down all the way to the

sanctuary of the shower. With needles of hot water scouring off the sticky fruit juice, she knew what she had to do. She would tell John David, and probably Sara, too—but not tonight. She needed to know more. She had to find out what Ria was refusing to do.

Maybe her people simply wanted her to drop it all and go back home. But the prickling in Elen's skin told her it was more than that. Caledon was up to something dire—something that would not only break the truce, it would start the war all over again, and make it much worse.

As always. When had Caledon ever done anything else?

Elen had grown up in a royal court, where everyone had secrets. She was much better than she sometimes wanted to be at watching and spying and being prepared to leap the instant she found something solid to leap on.

It was hard. She wanted to be a warrior, but for this she had to be a hunter. She had to lie in the covert and wait for the prey to come to her—to do something that would convince John David for once and for all that Caledon could never, ever be trusted.

For two days, nothing happened. Elen was

absolutely sure of that: she had not slept for more than a handful of minutes since she found Ria in the ramada. She was gravel-eyed and dizzy with lack of sleep.

This was not going to work. She needed help. There was one logical person who might be willing, if Elen asked her in the right way. Sara was John David's niece. She knew both of the hostages. He would listen to her.

Then, having overslept and found herself in the cabin all alone, Elen dragged herself to the lodge for breakfast and heard Lilly say inside, "How's it going? Getting any better?"

"Not much," Sara answered. "It's still all hate, all the time."

"You'd think they'd have eased up by now," Nick said. "They're so much alike it's not funny."

"That's probably why they hate each other so much," said Sara. She paused, sipping milk or juice from the sound. When she spoke again, her voice had lowered in a way that told Elen Ria was somewhere nearby, probably in the kitchen. "Ria would back down if she got the chance. She was willing to try when she came, until she got slammed in the face once too often. The other one is like Max when you put a leg on him. No rhyme, no reason, and God help you if you try to make her stop."

"I can understand, a bit," Lilly said. "All that about

her father, and how she grew up thinking he just up and left when he really was dead—that's not easy to get over."

"*She's* not getting over it," Sara said. "She's bound and determined that the enemy is the enemy, and she'll never in this life admit that anything good can come out of Caledon."

"I don't get that at all," said Nick.

Others murmured assent: they must all be there, all the campers from Earth. Sara said, "It's like brain lock. Uncle John thinks it's possible to unlock a whole world and make it see things differently. Maybe Caledon can do it. Ymbria? If they're all like her, this war will outlast the heat death of the universe."

Elen turned and walked away. She walked all the way to the guest barn, where there was a manure cart waiting and a line of stalls to clean and a bottle of water in the cooler in the tack room, for when she started to realize how unwise it had been to work in the heat without any liquid in her.

"That's what they think of me," she said to the horse whose stall she was cleaning. It happened to be Max, who was in with a bruised hoof. "I guess that's what I am. The one who'll never stop hating, because I'm not capable of stopping. It's just too bad I happen to be right."

Max slurped up water from his barrel and slobbered it all over her, then went back to what was left of his breakfast hay. Elen stood and dripped and thought about giving it all up and running away—really, this time. If she died doing it, who would care? Not anyone at Rancho Estrella, that was clear.

"No," she said, digging in with the manure and pitching another pile into the cart. "She's going down. If I go down with her, I don't care. I'll make them see what she really is."

No one asked Elen why she had skipped breakfast to clean stalls. No one had much to say to her at all. She hoped they felt guilty for talking about her behind her back, but she doubted it. She was in a fine, black mood.

That was Sunday, the second day of the weekend, which meant that after morning chores everyone had the afternoon off. The boys caught a ride to town with Francisco and another of the hands.

The Earth part of the tribe debated an expedition to something called a mall, which seemed to be a sort of bazaar, but decided to shut themselves up in the lodge with a stack of horse films instead. Elen would have liked to see the bazaar, but the lodge was cool and the films were almost as good as real horses, even if she had to watch them with a group of people who hated her. She especially liked the one about the war and the white stallions—some of them reminded her of Blanca—and the one about the girl who rode a wild race across a field of very high fences. That was an exploit worthy of a song in Ymbria.

She thought about making one, but her head still ached from lack of sleep. It was as much as she could do to keep an eye on Ria.

Ria seemed to have pushed all her troubles out of her mind. When the week began again with chores and riding and lessons and a ride down in the washes in the almost-cool evening, she was almost the person she had been on the first day: bright, smiling, traveling in the middle of the pack.

Elen was tired enough by then that she almost fell into the trap. For a brief, unguarded moment, she actually thought that Ria was someone she could like. She was glad she knew how false it was. The real Ria was a plotter in the dark. When that person came out again, she would betray them all.

On the fourth day after Elen saw clearly what Ria was, the weather broke at last. Morning chores were a sweaty misery. What riding anyone did, they did as soon as it was light, because by the time the sun was fully up, so was the heat.

In the late morning, the clouds piled up as they did every day, but today there were more of them and they piled higher. By early evening, lessons in the lodge needed a lamp or two, because the day had gone so dark.

Lightning lashed the mountaintops. Down below, the wind began to blow.

Elen heard it rattling the roof tiles and gusting in the eaves. Megan was teaching them about feeding horses, with numbers and calculations and this vitamin and that mineral and how much and what kind and how and when and how much to feed. Elen was good with numbers and could add them up faster in her head than the Earthlings could click them out on their calculators, but today she was distracted.

She wanted to be outside, with the wind in her hair and the tang of lightning in her nostrils. When she closed her eyes, she could see Blanca galloping through the wind and thunder and, as the first drops drummed on the roof, the grey veils of rain. She could feel the mare's delight, her joy in the storm, with its wildness and its beauty and its power.

It was like her. That was why she loved it.

By the time Elen swam up out of her half-dream, they were all ignoring Megan and looking toward the windows. She growled at them but let them go. "I'll let you off early today," she said, "but you'll pay tomorrow. Go on, celebrate. The monsoons are here!"

After all that, she was the first one out into the rain, with her arms wide and her head back and the cold wonderful streams of it running down her face and body.

Nick hung back under the porch roof, protesting. "There's lightning! We'll all get fried."

"Not today," said Sara, dancing past him. The rain by now was like a river set on end, coming down thick enough to drown in. They were all, except Nick, wringing wet and grinning.

The storm rolled away almost as fast as it had come, leaving behind a vanishing flock of rivulets and a brief but glorious breath of cool air. The smell of it was astonishing: sharp and strangely dry, nothing at all like rain anywhere else. Even after the sun came back, the day was not quite so hot; and there were more storms coming, more clouds turning black over the mountains.

Elen's shirt was already drying, and her hair was escaping its braid and springing into ringlets. She wrung as much water out of it as she could. Lilly and Nan were lucky: their thick black hair was cut short. Sara's was so straight that nothing could shift it.

Ria had not come out with the rest. One would think she would be even gladder of rain than the rest of them, but she stayed under the roof even after Nick scraped up his courage to come out. She flinched at every crack of thunder.

She was afraid. Or guilty, maybe. Afraid the lightning would strike her for all her people's sins.

The boys had no such problem. They wanted to go

for a ride to celebrate the rain, but Megan put a stop to that. "Nobody rides a steel-shod horse out here when there's lightning," she said, "and those nice sandy tracks you like to ride on can turn to racing rivers and sweep you away in seconds."

Matt and Lucas grumbled and seemed to give way. But the way their eyes were darting, they had a plan, and Megan had done little to convince them it was foolish. "We'll stay out of the washes," she heard Matt mutter to Lucas, "and keep an eye on the lightning. You with me?"

"After dinner," Lucas agreed.

Nick and the girls were not invited. Elen thought about telling Megan. But that would be dishonorable.

Her glance crossed Sara's. Sara nodded slightly. She had heard, too. She would take care of it, her eyes said.

Just two days ago Elen would have smiled and nodded back. Today she knew what Sara really thought of her. She replied with a flat stare, turned and went to the cabin to change into dry clothes and try to convince her hair to cooperate.

Ria did not want any dinner. She curled up on her bunk with her hands over her ears, hiding from the thunder.

Elen was happy to leave her to it, but Sara took a

plate to her from the dining room. Elen stayed in the lodge. There was studying to do, and a film when they were done. After that they all sat on the porch, watching the play of lightning down the valley. None of them was eager to close herself up in a cabin.

Finally Megan chased them all off to bed. "Morning doesn't stop coming early because you stayed up late," she said.

Sara still had her eyes on Matt and Lucas, and dragged her feet back to the cabin. Elen followed equally slowly, because the longer it took her to cross the square, the less time she would have to spend near Ria. Better yet, if the boys decided to go on their ride after all, she might delay another hour or more. Ria was going nowhere tonight, if Elen was any judge. She was much too terrified of a little thunder.

Sure enough, the boys' door opened and shut and a light went on—but Elen's eyes were sharp enough in the dark to see the two shadows that slipped out the back and slunk away toward the barn.

Or they tried to. Before they even reached the wall, they ran straight into Sara and Elen.

"On your way to get electrocuted?" Sara asked.

"There's no lightning around here," Lucas said. "It's all up on the mountain."

"It comes down fast enough when it wants to," Sara said. "Not that I care what happens to you, but those are my uncle's horses you're trying to kill."

Matt scoffed. "Nobody's going to kill any horses."

"Good!" Sara said promptly. "Here, we'll walk you back to your cabin. Unless you'd rather stop and say hello to Uncle John?"

Lucas made a strangled sound. Matt was less easily cowed. "You wouldn't tell."

"Oh, wouldn't I? You're going to steal a couple of horses and risk getting them drowned or struck by lightning. You bet I'll tell."

That backed them both down. They might not care about the horses, but they cared about being sent home. Elen was happy to play hired muscle and escort them to their door, then make sure they stayed where they were supposed to be.

CHAPTER II

Ria was not in the cabin when Elen and Sara came in. Her bunk was rumpled but empty, and her boots were missing from the pile by the door.

Elen said a word a princess in Ymbria was not supposed to know. She pushed past Sara toward the closet and the chest of drawers.

Everything that belonged to Ria was still there, except a jacket that she had never needed in the heat.

"My day pack's gone," Sara said behind her.

Elen turned. "What was in it?"

"Nothing much," said Sara. "A bottle for water. A bag of trail mix."

"She could have raided the kitchen," Elen said, more to herself than to Sara.

"Or just packed up the food I brought her from dinner." Sara shook her head. "I should have seen this coming."

"I did," Elen said, "but you wouldn't have listened to me. Everybody knows I'm all about the hate."

Sara winced. That was satisfying. But she said, "She's not the monster you think she is."

"No?"

Elen should have resisted the urge to say anything. Sara's face had closed. "You stay here," she said. "I mean it. Stay. I'll go find her."

"In the dark? With lightning?"

"I was born on this ranch," Sara said. "I know every inch of it. Wherever she's got to, I'll find her."

"What if she's not on the ranch?" Elen asked. "What if she's on the worldroad?"

"She can't do that," said Sara. "Not without a world-runner."

"I did."

"From Ymbria," Sara said. "This is Rancho Estrella. Nobody comes or goes from here unless there's a world-runner to guide her."

"Maybe," said Elen. "Maybe not. Either way, John David needs to know she's missing."

"Uncle John has enough to worry about. If I can't find her by morning, I'll tell him. I'm sure she's somewhere nearby—probably hanging with the horses. She's not crazy like the boys. She won't tempt the lightning. You saw how afraid of it she was."

"Was she? What is a Caledonian's first and greatest skill? Lying. She planned this. I heard her. The night of the team penning, in the ramada, she used the fountain to talk to her people. They wanted her to do something. She said she wouldn't. What if she was lying to them, too?"

Sara's eyes had gone wider with each word Elen spoke. "Why? What would she do?"

"I don't know," Elen said. "Something bad. That's all I could tell."

"That's a lot of help," Sara said. She kicked off her sneakers and sat to pull on her boots.

Elen did the same. Sara glowered. Elen stared flatly back.

"Look," said Sara with careful patience, "it's not that I don't appreciate your company, but I don't need to play referee for the war of the worlds tonight. Stay here and get some sleep. I'll bring Ria back as soon as I find her."

Elen sucked in a breath and let it go in a rush. "What if you don't find her? What if she's found a way to get off the ranch—or Caledon has?"

Sara paused. "You mean they've found a way in?"

"They've got one of their own here."

"No," Sara said. "No, that can't happen. We have

defenses that no world can break. The power of Faerie itself sustains them."

Elen tried not to sound defensive, but it was hard. "When she was in the ramada, she talked about how desperate they are and how she couldn't do whatever it was. They yelled so loud I could hear it, though I couldn't catch what they said. Then she cut them off."

"I'm sure that's what you thought you heard," Sara said, "but—"

"I'm not from Caledon. I don't tell lies!"

Elen pressed her hand to her mouth. Screaming did no one any good. It only convinced Sara that Elen was incapable of being rational about Ria.

"Look," Elen said. "Let me help you hunt. I promise I won't do anything violent if we find her. I'll let your people take care of that."

"I don't think—" Sara began.

"I'll go to John David," Elen said, "and tell him you went out alone after lights out."

That was a low blow, but it hit the target. "All *right*! You can come. But keep quiet and don't try to get in the way when we catch up with her. Do you understand?"

"Perfectly," Elen said.

The air between them was not friendly as they ventured back out into the damp and sticky dark, but Elen was hard put to care. Sara insisted on searching the Earth side of the ranch. Well enough. Let her do that.

She went on foot. Elen thought of pointing out that Ria was probably on horseback, but after all, Sara had made her promise not to interfere.

The storms that had moved off earlier were coming back, rolling along the ridges. The wind gusted now warm and now cool. Their noses were full of the fierce dry smell of rain in the desert.

"Greasewood bush," Sara said as Elen stopped to breathe deep. "And dust and sage. And a little lightning."

It was a truce of sorts. Sara paused to let Elen move up beside her.

They were halfway down the path to the guest barn. So far there was no sign of Ria. Everything was quiet except for the growl of the thunder. The barn dogs must be asleep: none of them barked when Sara slipped through the back door.

All the horses were in their stalls or else in their pens under the half-roof, asleep or finishing off the last of their bedtime hay. None of the ones that Ria would be likely to take was missing. Even Sharif was safe in his corner pen, though he seemed less happy than the others: he was pacing in circles and peering off into the dark.

"He's always like this in thunderstorms," Sara said. He came to touch her palm with his nose and blow in her face, but he ignored Elen completely.

"Maybe he's looking for Ria," Elen said. Not that she believed it, but she was feeling odd. Somewhere between the barn and Sharif's pen, she had started to itch, as if something inside her skull was trying to get out. It felt like Blanca, but when she reached for the familiar presence, it moved off. She tried not to feel rejected, but it was hard.

Sara darted away in the direction in which Sharif was staring. Elen squawked in protest—she had not meant Sara to act on what she said—but Sara was already halfway down the slope into the wash. Elen slipped and scrambled after her.

That part of the wash was always full of footprints: the dogs hunted rabbits up and down the channel, and riders used it to get to the hill trails. There was no way to tell if Ria had gone that way.

Elen was sure she had not. They were going in the wrong direction. The itch behind her eyes was pushing her away from this place.

"Blanca?" she asked, calling softly into the dark. No answer came back.

Sara went down as far as the first turn, but before she could go on, a bolt of lightning struck the hilltop directly above them. In that searingly bright instant, Elen saw her face, pale and startled, and something else behind her: a line of big dark shapes cantering up into the sky.

Worldrunners were riding out in force—at least a score of them, and maybe more. Elen had never seen that many together. They always came to Ymbria in ones and twos.

"She's not here," Sara said in the dark after the glare of lightning. "Let's go back."

Elen had been going to tell Sara about the riders, but Sara's voice sounded so small in the wide world that Elen decided to wait until they were somewhere well lit and safe. They turned back in silence and clambered up again into the line of pens. Sharif was still pacing, and the rest of the horses were still mostly asleep.

Sara might have gone back through the barn, but Elen needed to see what was on the other side. That need was part of the oddness in her head.

The stallions went out in paddocks at night, and the mares went inside. The red stallion and the spotted one were pacing as Sharif had been, biting the bars and shaking their heavy heads. Elen walked quickly toward the paddock on the end, the one nearest the mesquite grove.

It was empty. Moondance was gone.

That did not have to mean anything bad. Either he was in the barn or he had been moved back to the part of the ranch where his kind belonged.

Elen tried to call to Blanca again, silently this time. Blanca was not answering. Whatever she was doing, it left her no time to talk to Elen.

She was probably on the worldroads, carrying a rider wherever a whole troop of them had had to go.

Elen made herself focus on the world around her and see what there was to see. There were only mares in the stalls. No big-headed grey stallion.

Elen spun around in the barn aisle, nearly knocking Sara off her feet. "Moondance isn't broken to ride, is he?"

Sara frowned. "Bran started him in the spring. He's awfully green. You don't think—"

"Why was he here?" Elen demanded. "What was he doing?"

"He was breeding mares," Sara said. "What else would he be doing in the stud barn?"

"Look," Elen said with tight-strained patience. "I know what he is. He's a worldrunner. Just tell me the truth. Why was he here and not where he belongs?"

Sara blinked. Elen watched her decide not to waste any more time. "We do that every year. Crossing worldrunners on the other horses doesn't always work, but when it does, it's worth it." She frowned at Elen. "He must have gone back."

"Yes," said Elen. "He must have. Because if he didn't—"

Her voice trailed off, but the rest of it unwound in her head. Because if he had not, that must be the bad thing, the thing that Caledon had forced Ria to do. Somehow, they had found a way to steal a worldrunner from the very heart of Earth, from the House of the Star itself.

When Elen opened the gate to the other half of the ranch, she heard Sara's gasp behind her. "You're not supposed to know that's there!"

Elen turned in the gate. The air on the other side was the same as the air she had been walking through all that night: dark, damp, and full of thunder. "Are you coming or aren't you?"

"I can't," Sara said. "Neither can you. Not if we want to stay in camp."

"So stay." Elen turned her back on Sara and stepped through the gate.

Sacrifices in stories were more dramatic, with longer speeches, and usually involved weapons. This was just a sandy path down a hill and across a wash and toward the worldriders' barn. Elen did pause to wonder why she was doing this, but the answer was clear enough. Whatever Ria was up to, it must involve a worldrunner. Bringing down Caledon was worth almost anything. Saving a worldrunner made it really and truly and absolutely worth doing.

Halfway across the wash, Sara matched her step for step. She was breathing hard, and not only because she had run a fair way in damp sand. "You think Ria went this way, too?"

Elen decided not to say anything about what Sara had just done to herself. "I think worldrunners know where Moondance is," she said.

She did not wait to see or hear what Sara thought of that. She turned back toward the dark and trotted the rest of the way across the wash. Her feet knew where to step, though she had only been this way twice. Gradually her eyes adapted. There was thunder everywhere, and lightning lacing the sky. She was insane to be out in it, but the need to see Blanca had taken hold of her somewhere between the gate and the dry riverbed. It was getting stronger with every breath she took.

She stopped even trying to fight it, and let it pull her up out of the wash toward the barn. There were no lights in the upper story tonight, except for a lone, dim one on the end. The lower part was completely dark.

Most of the stalls were empty. Blanca was still there: Elen could feel her, and hear her whicker as they walked quickly by. There was a strong sense about her of waiting; and another sense, nearly strong enough to hear as words. *Almost time. Almost.*

Elen wanted to stop and ask that that meant, but she was afraid of losing Sara. Sara was already most of the way down the aisle. Elen caught up with her just as she opened a door at the end and flipped on a light. Rows of saddle racks lined the walls. Most had names on them, but no saddles or bridles. Only a handful of saddles were left in the room. There must have been forty of them missing from the racks.

The rack with Blanca's name still had a saddle on it. So did the one above it, labeled HERA. There was no rack for Moondance.

"Something's happened," Sara said. Then she answered the question Elen had been going to ask: "This many riders never go out at once."

It was her turn to spin and bolt, and Elen's to run after her. She ran past Blanca's stall and the veterinary stall with the badly burned mare still in it, still alive and moving, but the rider and his cot were gone. Sara burst out of the riders' barn and aimed for the breeding barn, with the mares' and foals' pasture stretching out beyond it in the lightning-punctuated dark.

The pasture was empty. Six mares were in the barn, not happily: they pawed and called when Elen and Sara came in. Elen looked, but none of the mares was pregnant. They all had foals in the stalls with them.

She tried to remember how many pregnant mares

there had been when Blanca came off the worldroad and dropped her in the water tank. Three? Four? Where would they be, if not here or in the main barn?

Sara spun completely around. Her eyes were wild. "The mares are gone. Nobody ever—how could they—the pregnant mares are gone!"

CHAPTER 12

Elen's knees tried to fail and drop her in a heap on the floor. She refused to give in to them. She propped herself against the wall.

This was the crime that Caledon had wanted to commit in the very beginning: to steal worldrunners and breed them away from Earth. "But," she said, "everyone knows it can't be done. Worldrunners can't foal safely off Earth. What does Caledon think it can do to change that?"

Sara blinked as if she had forgotten who Elen was. "Caledon? How do you know that's who it was?"

Elen tried not to spit, but she could not keep the

scorn out of her voice. "Oh, come! Ria was arguing with her people about some horrible thing they wanted her to do. Now she's missing, Moondance and a herd of mares are gone, just about every worldrunner who is fit to ride is out on the roads, and you still think it could be anyone else?"

"It could be," Sara insisted. "She might have sensed it somehow and taken it into her head to stop it. That would be like her sense of honor."

Elen really did spit then. "Caledonian honor. They're all bandits and thieves."

Sara ignored her. "The riders will track her down and find her if she's out on the roads. We should go back and try to sleep—in case somebody needs us later. Or tomorrow."

"What would they think they need us for?" Elen wanted to know. "They'll expect us to sit down, keep quiet, and stay out of the way."

"Yes," Sara said. She said it a little more slowly than she might have. "You're not thinking—"

"It's perfectly sensible," Elen said. "All those riders and all those worldrunners have to be able to find her. Right? They'll probably look in Caledon first, and that's where she probably went."

"But?" said Sara.

There was not supposed to be a but. Elen was not supposed to be thinking that Ria was part of the tribe, and the tribe should go after her. The riders would not know how Moondance had gone to Ria the day the campers did stall duty in the breeding barns, nor would they know how Ria had argued against some terrible thing that her people wanted to do. If they caught her, they might do something terrible to her.

None of it made enough sense to say aloud. It hardly made sense in Elen's head. "We have to go after her," she said.

"Oh, no," said Sara. "There's no way. Riders train for years before they travel the roads. Even for them it's horribly dangerous. People die out there."

"I didn't," Elen said.

Sara shook her head. She was barely listening. "That's why it's forbidden for any of us to ride a world-runner. To steal one and go on a chase like this? You can go back home and be a princess and forget you ever came to Earth. I live here. This is where I was born. I've wanted to be a rider for as long as I've been alive. I can't give it all up. I can't."

There was not much Elen could say to that. Really, Sara was right. Forty riders had gone hunting. What could two completely untrained girls do, except get in the way?

There was one thing. The itch in Elen's head had opened up into the full force of Blanca's presence. She was done with waiting. She banged against the door of her stall, loudly and imperiously. *In. Now. Get me ready. It's time to ride.*

Elen's head was splitting, between Sara's bitter logic and Blanca's eruption of impatience. "You go," she said to Sara. "Get away before anybody knows you're here. You," she said to Blanca, "stop kicking inside my head. I'm moving as fast as I can."

Blanca barely muted her uproar. Sara stared at Elen as if she had been speaking Ymbrian, which she knew she had not. She was not that far gone.

"She *talks* to you?"

"She does something to me," Elen said.

She dived through the door into the tack room, snatched saddle and bridle and a bucket of brushes, and set about giving Blanca what she wanted so badly.

Sara babbled at her. She half-listened while she brushed Blanca. "You can't do this. You're out of your mind. How can you—"

"Somebody has to," Elen said between the saddle pad and the saddle. The saddle was a bit of a challenge: it was hung with two water bottles—both of which sloshed heavily—and a pair of saddlebags full of who knew what. Blanca was fussing too much to let Elen look.

She settled the saddle on Blanca's back and reached under the wide white barrel for the girth. Blanca shook her mane and pawed. *Faster!*

Elen was moving as fast as she could. "Stop wiggling," she said to Blanca. Blanca stopped—for half a breath. Then she was pawing and fussing again.

The girth was tight. Blanca lunged for the bit and nearly caught Elen's fingers. Elen smacked her without thinking, then froze, horrified. Blanca barely noticed.

The instant all the buckles were fastened, Blanca was in motion. Elen just managed to catch the reins before the mare bulled through the stall door. By the time she reached the door to the outside, she was halfway to a trot.

Elen let the force of Blanca's speed sweep her up and into the saddle. She crossed the stableyard in two long strides; then she was in among the trees.

The mesquite grove was black dark. When lightning flashed, it barely touched the topmost branches, and cast no light below. Elen ducked low over Blanca's neck and let the mare carry her, weaving through rough and spiny branches.

A pale glimmer brought Elen's head up. The wash ran past the far edge of the grove. Shadows bunched together in it. Then one moved in just the right direction, and Elen saw a horse's head and ears, and the faint glint of white on its forehead.

They were moving away down the wash. Elen could see just well enough to count five of them. It was too dark to see if any had a rider. The shiver down her spine said one did.

Clever Ria, letting all the riders scatter on the world-roads while she hid her theft in plain sight.

If it was Ria. Elen had to allow the thought, but even as it drifted past, she knew she was right.

The mares were still on Earth. That was not so bad, was it? Especially if Elen could somehow talk Ria into putting them back. Or Sara could. Then nobody need know what had really happened. It would all look like a false alarm, and neither Sara nor the hostages would have been anywhere near it.

While Elen's mind ran on, Blanca quickened her pace from walk to trot. The track beneath her hooves was perfectly straight.

So was the one the mares were following. They looked suddenly much farther away than they had. Blanca gathered her haunches to lift into a canter.

Another horse surged up beside her. It was dark, with a white star. That must be Hera: her saddle had been the only one left besides the saddles that belonged to the wounded worldrunners. Sara's face was just recognizable above the mare's narrow black head.

"I'm not going back," Elen said.

"I know," said Sara. "I'm going with you."

"You changed your mind?"

There was no way to read an expression on that pale blur of face, but Sara's tone was dry. "We're not all as stubborn as you."

"You can't go after her. You know what will happen if you do."

"We have to," Sara said. "Nobody else knows where she is."

"Do we?"

"Blanca and Hera do," Sara said.

"You said it yourself," said Elen. "We're not trained riders."

"There aren't any left," Sara said. "They're all out chasing moonbeams."

Elen's head was throbbing. She could barely shape the words, let alone the thoughts behind them. "You stay here. Try to find John David, if he's not out riding himself, and tell him what's happened. I'll follow Ria."

"You can't go alone," Sara said. "That's one rule I won't break, because it's the only way we have any hope of either finding her or keeping ourselves safe."

"Blanca will keep me safe," Elen said.

Sara ignored that. "I left a note for Uncle John. He'll do what he'll do. So will we. We've got to move fast now, before we lose her, and hope we can catch her and get both her and the mares back before it's too late. They're all right around due date. If one or more of them tries to foal out there—"

"The babies will die." Elen's throat was tight. This would finish Caledon, and Ymbria would have had nothing to do with it. She could turn back, save herself and Sara, let it happen.

But if she did that, worldrunners would die.

Sara had made her choice. Blanca had never had to make one.

"Why do you even need me?" Elen demanded.

The answer came not in words but in pictures: a shining white shape that looked vaguely like a horse with a rider on her back. They were not two separate beings. They were one. The larger part was strong and wise and had the worldroads in its bones. The smaller one was clever and quick and could think around corners.

They needed each other. Blanca could follow a straight track and keep it safe, but she needed the rider to get where she wanted to go. The rider's mind had a different kind of focus. That was Elen's part.

"But I'm not trained!"

Blanca was. She wanted Elen. Elen fit. The image that came with that was like a good saddle that was made for the horse, that sat just right on her back. It was important that Elen fit.

"I don't understand," Elen said.

Don't understand. Ride.

"I can do that," Elen said. She felt light suddenly, almost dizzy. Her headache had gone away. She could make a grand speech, or she could stop dragging her feet and say, "Let's go, then."

CHAPTER 13

It took all the trust Elen had to sit quietly on Blanca's back and let her go where she was so desperate to go, following the track of the pregnant mares. The road was pale ahead of them, sandy and level and perfectly straight.

The storm broke over their heads. Blanca took no notice. Cold rain streamed down Elen's face and soaked her shirt and jeans.

Lightning struck *up* from the mountains, branching like a tree, spreading across the whole sky. The branches of it were purple and lavender and pink and blinding white. Clouds boiled behind them.

There were things in the clouds, gaunt and bony shapes of horses and hounds. A man rode in front of them all, tall and broad-shouldered, and his head was the head of a stag, with antlers that spread across half the sky. A long line of shadowy riders galloped behind him, leaping through the lightning.

Elen was cold from the inside out. The Wild Hunt, the guardians of Faerie, had come to Earth. They only left the bounds of the enchanted realm for the greatest need or the most dreadful crime. That was how terrible this theft of worldrunners was.

She looked back over her shoulder. Sara's face was dead white.

The lightning died; the rain passed on by. The dark wrapped around them. Elen could no longer see the Wild Hunt, but she could hear it.

If she had been lying in the cabin, drifting off to sleep, she might have taken it for coyotes. Out there, with the rain blowing away and the thunder rolling, it was nothing like that familiar desert song.

Lightning flashed again, and Elen froze all the way to the marrow. The wide, flat road was gone. They perched on a ridge that jutted up out of the desert. There was nothing but space on either side of the narrow trail. If she had tried to dismount, she would have fallen half a thousand feet to the rocky wash below.

Elen did not like heights. At all. She clutched

Blanca's mane and squeezed her eyes shut and tried not to shake.

Blanca walked forward. Hera's footsteps were like an echo of hers, lighter and a little quicker, following close behind. "Breathe," Elen said to herself. "Breathe."

She dared not faint. If she did, she would slip off Blanca's back and fall. And fall, and fall, and . . .

Blanca was perfectly calm, as if she walked the knife's edge every day. Was this a sword bridge? Elen wondered. If it was not, she never wanted to know what a real one was like.

Blanca tracked her sisters by the memory that they left behind, a faint shimmer in the worldroad, the hint of disturbance that to her was as clear as a fresh scent to a hound. When Elen focused on it, she could pick out four separate strands, and a fifth that was darker. That one smelled of stallion.

Blanca started down a slope that was steep enough to make Elen's breath catch. All she could do was hold on and try not to lose what little self-control she had left.

Something shone faintly ahead of her. It was a grey horse. Elen could just see the shadows of others in front of it.

Blanca let out a soft snort. The squealing rumble that answered it belonged to a stallion.

Elen knew who it had to be. It must be Moondance.

He had a rider on his back. Elen saw the pale blur of a face, then it turned and disappeared. Moondance spurted away.

In the instant before Elen clamped heels to Blanca's sides, both mares sprang in pursuit.

Something caught Elen's eye and drew it upward. Jagged mountains rose up over her. They were much, much closer than they should have been.

Her mind acknowledged then what her body had known since before the rain began. They were still on Earth, still riding through the mountains above Rancho Estrella, but they were on a worldroad. Its power already surrounded them, shortening distances, bringing together places that were leagues apart.

Blanca's gallop was smooth and her breathing easy. She kept Moondance at precisely the same distance, no matter how fast or slow he went.

The road was wider now, and steeper, winding upward. The mountains were even closer. There was no mortal way they could have come so close so fast.

That thought had barely left Elen's head when Blanca ran straight through the sheer and stony slopes. They felt like mist and fog, and smelled like cold iron.

Things moved in the fog. They made Elen feel cold and small and scared. If she looked at them, or even caught a glimpse of what they looked like, she knew that she would shrivel away to nothing.

She buried her face in Blanca's mane. That saved her eyes, but her ears had no defenses.

The growls and shrieks were bad. The whispering was worse. It sounded like hissing snakes, but it had words in it, words Elen could not understand. She only knew that, whatever the whisperers were, they were no friends to her or anyone like her.

She almost wept when they came out of the fog into starlight. There was no storm there. The mountains were sharp-edged and high, but they were different mountains than the ones that rose above Rancho Estrella.

Blanca's footfalls had been almost silent, slipping and scraping on sand. Suddenly they were loud, clattering on rocks and sending pebbles flying down the steep track.

Something had gone down ahead of them, plowing a path through the sand and stones. Elen hoped they were following the mares—and the thief who had stolen them.

The air felt different. It was cooler, wetter; it smelled of green things and distant rain. The stars blurred overhead, half-veiled by streamers of cloud.

"Sara," she said, faint and hoarse as if she had not used her voice in eons. "Please tell me we're still somewhere on Earth."

"I don't think we are," Sara said. "I don't know. I've sneaked looks at the maps, but I never memorized them. I didn't think I'd have to till I was in school to be a worldrider."

"I have a map," said Elen. "It's in my coat pocket. In the closet. I never even stopped to think—"

"We didn't, did we?" Sara said. Her tone was wry. "All I remember is the one that said, and it meant it: *Here Be Dragons.*"

Elen looked up before she thought. There were no sinuous shapes coiling in the sky, and no gouts of flame.

But there was something moving on the road ahead. Horses in a herd, trotting behind the pale shimmer of their leader.

Blanca kept to the same pace she had set since she started following Moondance. She was calm, alternating between trot and canter, with intervals of big, free-swinging walk. However strange this road was to Elen and Sara, to her it was as familiar as her own pasture.

"Where are we?" Elen asked her.

Blanca's answer translated to a single word: *Between.*

In between worlds. Down along the edges of Faerie. This place was as safe as between-places could be. It kept its shape as they passed through it, and nothing living or otherwise objected to their passage.

Elen found herself sliding into a half-dream. It was late and the day had been long; sleep kept threatening to ambush her. That was dangerous. If she slept, she would lose focus; and Blanca needed that focus to keep her on the track. She dared not give way to it.

She looked back. Sara was still there. Hera's star and the white blanket over her haunches shone eerily bright in starlight.

Just as Elen started to face front again, Sara nodded and swayed and started to slide. "*Sara!*" Elen called sharply.

The air rang like shaken silver. A name spoken in Faerie had power.

Sara jerked upright. Elen held her breath, but nothing came roaring out of the dark to devour them. The road was quiet again, and the stars shone down, white and cold.

This was not the road that had brought Elen to Earth. It had its moments of terror, but mostly it was wide and flat and, of course, straight. They came off the mountain into a wood of gnarled and thickset trees.

Ria was too much of a horse person to pick up speed when the track was level—not with pregnant mares to think of. Blanca stayed at the same exact distance behind. When Elen tried to push her to close the gap, she refused. She was exactly where she should be.

The track ran straight through the trees into a long rolling expanse of grass, silvered in starlight. A soft wind played across it, rippling it like a sea.

When Elen looked back to the track, it was empty and open ahead. There were no horses on it. There was nowhere for them to go, and yet they were gone.

Elen tried to halt Blanca, but the mare ignored her.

"Do you see them?" Elen asked Sara.

"No," Sara answered. "What should I see?"

Her voice sounded faint and far away, as if she spoke out of a dream.

Elen went cold. In Faerie, everything was magic and nothing could be trusted; dreams came to life and no single thing was solid or steady or stable. Faerie was the most dangerous place of all.

They should be safe as long as they stayed on the track. Elen told herself that, and did her best to believe it.

Ria was somewhere on this track. She had to be. Through Blanca she caught again the sense of the worldrunners moving ahead, but it was faint. It needed to be closer.

She squeezed her eyes shut. In her mind she pictured Ria as clearly as she could, and Moondance—that was clearer; he was a horse, after all. Ria was only a human.

Wherever Moondance was, Blanca had to go. Elen filled her whole mind with that, and her heart, and every part of her that she could reach. No matter what spells were at work in this place or what tricks or deceptions Caledon had made to baffle pursuit, Elen had one great advantage: she was part of a tribe, the tribe of horse girls. And so was Ria.

John David was right. Caledon had outsmarted it-self. Elen was going to be the one who proved it.

CHAPTER 14

Elen opened her eyes. She had felt the air change again, growing even damper and colder.

Blanca carried her through a wilderness of thorns. All around the straight track, branches grew so close they interwove, and spines grew into spines. Nothing at all could get in—except tiny birds flashing as bright as jewels in the rising sun, darting in and out through the bristling branches.

Elen looked back. Hera was still there, and Sara mute and pale. The thorns had closed in behind them. The only way out was through.

Elen swallowed the uprush of panic. They were

going to die. The horses had finally had enough. They would kill off the humans who treated them like transportation, threw saddles on their backs and bits in their mouths and forced them to do foolish or insane things.

"*No!*" Elen said. The sound of her voice was as harsh in that place as a raven's croak. The tiny jeweled birds rose up in a swarm and fled. So did the dark thoughts. Blanca was warm and solid under her, not hating her, not wishing her ill at all.

Hera came up beside her. Sara was recovering from the spell that had bound her: her eyes could see again, though they were a little too wide and a little too dark. "What in the worlds was that?"

"Lies," she said. "Sleights of Faerie."

"I thought the roads were protected," Sara said.

"They are," said Elen. "That doesn't mean they're totally safe."

Sara shuddered. "What if we're following a lie? What if Ria didn't come this way at all?"

Her words rocked Elen in the saddle, but Elen shook her head so hard her braid whipped from side to side like a cat's tail. "It's not a lie! She is ahead of us. She's hiding somehow—a spell, an amulet, something that keeps us from seeing her, and anyone else from doing it, either. But we can follow her. If we're strong enough. If we can keep our minds focused."

"And if nothing hunts us down and kills us."

Elen hissed. "Don't talk like that! Try to keep her in your head and ride toward her."

"I know how it's supposed to work," Sara said. "Are you sure you do?"

"Better than you," Elen said. "We have to be perfectly clear, and not get distracted. We have to *know* what we're riding to."

"What if we can't?"

"Faerie swallows us up forever."

It was meant to be a bitter joke, but the truth of it rang in her skull. The forest of thorns rippled and shimmered. Elen felt the fabric of Faerie fraying around her.

She fixed her eyes on Blanca's ears and her mind on Ria's face. Something pressed on her hip, niggling at her until she reached into her pocket to pull out whatever it was.

It was the medallion she had won at the team penning, still on its bright blue ribbon. The mountain on one side and the star on the other gleamed at her in the strange pale light of Faerie.

It was only a disk of bronze, common and ordinary and perfectly unmagical. And yet it made her think of the talisman she had brought from Ymbria. That had had no magic, either, but she had been able to use it to guide her for a while, until the road grew too strong for her little skill.

There might be no magic in the medallion, but the

Mountain and the Star were great powers among the worlds. Their images anchored her. The magic of Earth was in them, strong and quiet. It matched the magic that was in Blanca.

She looked past the cast bronze to Sara's rounded ivory face and her deep eyes. They had gone quiet, too, as if the medallion was as much a talisman for her as for Elen.

Maybe it was more. She belonged to the House of the Star. She was part of its magic, too.

"We can do this," Elen said. "We're a tribe, remember? We belong together."

"Even you and Ria?"

"Nobody has to like everybody in the tribe," Elen said.

Sara bent her head to that. She knew how huge a thing that was. "Let's go find her," she said.

CHAPTER 15

They found the first sign of Ria in a world of green. Everywhere green. Tall trees and emerald-green undergrowth and shimmery things flitting through it on green wings.

It was cool. There was water: a brook ran across the road. Blanca pulled the reins out of Elen's hands and dived down to drink.

Elen dismounted on the soft bank, slipping a little in the mud, and bent to scoop up water in her hands. As she paused, looking down, the surface stilled.

She let out a sound, not really a word, but it brought Sara up beside her. Sara's hiss of breath echoed her own.

The water was as smooth as glass. It looked like a mirror, but what it reflected was nothing like the green branches or the pale-green sky of the world around them.

They hung above the surface of a world, hovering like hawks in the grey and tumbled heaven. It was green below, almost painfully so, but in the rain-blurred distance she saw the black of charred and fire-blasted rock, littered with the shards of trees.

"Caledon," Elen said.

Sara tilted a glance at her. "How do you know?"

Blanca blew out a snort and shook her head, lowering it to rub an itch on her knee. "She told me," Elen said.

Sara frowned, but she did not argue. She bent to peer closer at the reflection in the water. A moment later, Elen did the same.

In the heart of the circle of green was a shape of grey stone, the outline of a wall and a clutter of roofs. It looked like a farmstead, tucked in a remote valley surrounded by desert, with a blue jewel of a lake to water it.

There were horses inside the wall. Elen counted four. There should be five, if they were stolen worldrunners. Or the fifth might be under one of the roofs.

A breath of wind blew over the stream. The water rippled and cleared. There was nothing in it but weeds and stones.

"That's where they are," Elen said. "It has to be."

"Are you sure?" asked Sara. "Would Caledon be that obvious? Wouldn't they hide what they've stolen somewhere else—preferably as far from their own world as possible?"

"I don't think they can," Elen said. "Everybody hates them. I can't imagine anyone giving them shelter after what they've done. If I were them, I'd go the other way. I'd hide in plain sight."

"But that's the first place anyone would think to look."

"Not if they've taken whatever magic is left in their world after all the wars, and used it to hide what they've stolen. We don't throw magic about in Ymbria. Only the best and most highly trained of us are allowed to work more than the simplest seeings and spells. Caledon lets its people do what they like with whatever they have or can find, no matter how wasteful or destructive that can be."

"If that's true, and they're working spells to hide what they're doing, how come we could see them?"

Elen had been wondering about that herself. She gave Sara the best answer she could. "We've tracked them from the start. We know exactly what they did. Everybody else has to be just guessing. We *know*."

"We know Ria," Sara said, nodding. "So now we go to Caledon."

"Now we go where Ria is," Elen said. She felt a need

to be precise. Some of it came from Blanca, and some was her instinct.

They filled their water bottles carefully, because there was no telling when they would pass by water again. Then they mounted, pulling themselves stiffly into the worldrunners' saddles.

Elen was almost sorry to leave this green and peaceful place. Then as Blanca began to move, she saw how a buzzing mass of tiny green winged things, halfway between a beetle and a hummingbird, had gathered under one of the trees. There was an animal there, a little like a cat and a little like a squirrel, with green fur that blended into the undergrowth. It flattened to the ground and tried to hide, but the winged things swarmed it.

Its blood was glistening green. It made no sound at all while it died. In the time it took Elen to open her mouth and suck in a breath, the animal disappeared. All that was left was a pile of greenish-white bones on the green leaves.

Elen gagged. "No wonder they call this the Road Perilous," she said. Her voice was thick; her throat burned. "If your Earth has gods, pray they keep us safe."

"Gods and worldrunners," Sara said.

Blanca's ear slanted back. Elen took the message as it was intended. Now was not the time to stop trusting her. Elen was following her gut, and her gut told her to keep on with this madness of a quest.

It was all but liquid with terror, but that only made her more determined. She was going to find Ria and get her back to Rancho Estrella and make very sure she paid for what she had done, or die trying.

When they rode out of the green world, Elen had the farmstead in Caledon in her mind, and Blanca strode out as if she knew where it was. But when Elen shied away from the thought of the road there and all its dangers, not to mention the sheer deadliness of Caledon itself, Blanca lost her willingness to go forward. The landscape around them blurred and started to flicker.

A cold, damp fog surrounded them. Elen listened for the voices and growling that she had heard inside the mountain, but there was nothing. Not a comforting absence of hostile beings, but *nothing*. Absolute, unbreakable silence.

When she looked back, Sara had started to fade. Hera still seemed solid, but her edges were dim.

Elen wrenched her mind back to the farmstead and the horses and the grey and stormy sky. Sara came into focus. The fog thinned. Blanca picked up speed.

Elen rubbed her neck. "What's happening? Why can't you do it yourself any more?"

Blanca did not answer, exactly. Instead Elen heard

Bran's voice in her head, sharp and clear, as if he stood directly behind her. She almost turned to look, but she knew there was no one there but Sara.

"Horses live in the present. I've seen smart ones plan things, like the mare who tracked down and kicked blue hell out of a snotty filly the day after the filly kicked *her*, but when they're out there doing what horses do, it's all about the now. If they think about time, it's about the past—running old tapes, or anticipating moves in a reining pattern because they've done the pattern before. It's humans who think in the future."

Blanca needed Elen to see what had not happened yet, or had not happened before, so that she could take them to it. As long as she was going home to Earth or following the clear track of her herdmates, she knew exactly what to do. Now that the trail had vanished and the only guide was an image that Elen had seen in a stream, she needed Elen to find the way.

She had the road in her blood. Elen had the future in her head.

That was why worldrunners needed riders—and why riders needed years of schooling before they even began. And yet here was Elen, after ten whole days in the House of the Star, trying to save a life that might not even be there to save.

If they found Ria alive and got her out of whatever tangle she had got herself into, she would owe them all, horses and riders, a tremendous debt. Elen would be collecting for years, if not for the rest of her life.

Supposing, of course, that any of them lived to do it.

They came out of the fog into midair. The road was a shaft of sunlight slanting sharply down into a city of bones.

The city was huge. It filled a valley scooped out of a mountain peak. There were rows of houses, walls and towers, and long avenues lined with pillars, all built of bones. Elen tried to imagine people living here, and her brain refused to do it. Unless they were bone people—skeletons, like the riders in the Wild Hunt.

It was a long, steep way down. Blanca almost had to sit down and slide the last hundred feet, into an avenue of bones.

The road evaporated. They were a good two man-lengths up, worse than any lover's leap Elen had thrown herself and her horse over. She wound her cold and shaking fingers in Blanca's mane and squeezed her eyes shut and tried not to curl up into a ball.

It was a long, long, long time to hang in the air, with her stomach in knots and her chest too tight to let her breathe.

176 ★ CAITLIN BRENNAN

Then they came down. The lurch was not as bad as she had braced for. Worse was the crunch of bones under the horses' hooves.

She sucked in air. It was dry and hot and tasted like burnt toast. It made her throat clench. Behind her she heard Sara retching.

A shadow fell across the light. She looked up into a lofty and terrible face crowned with antlers as wide as the sky.

CHAPTER 16

The Horned King looked down upon her from atop a hill of bones. Some of those about his feet stirred with a kind of life: skeletons of hounds with whitely gleaming fangs. His face like theirs was a skull—larger than that of a deer, with far wider antlers.

"Elk," Sara said out of the corner of her mouth. She had to swallow after she said it, but she seemed to have her stomach mostly under control. She rode Hera up beside Blanca and bowed over the mare's neck. "Great one," she said.

Elen felt as tiny and trembly and terrified as a mouse in front of a hawk. This was the great king, the lord of the Wild Hunt, the terrible power that held sway on the borders of Faerie. She managed to bow as Sara had, but it was more of a collapse.

Blanca stood perfectly still. Her head was up and her ears were pricked. She was alert, but if she was troubled, Elen could not feel it.

The Horned King bent his head in gracious acknowledgment. Deep inside the empty sockets of the skull, a pale light gleamed.

Elen's body could not move. Her mind thrashed and flailed. They were all going to die. The king's hounds would tear apart their bodies, and the Hunt would capture their souls.

"Good morning," the Horned King said.

His voice was deep and soft and perfectly civil. Elen sat immobile on Blanca's back, with her mouth open and no words in her head at all.

Sara had the presence of mind to respond, "And a fair morning to you, great one."

"It is not often that worldrunners pass through this city," the king said. "You honor it greatly."

Somehow Elen managed to find what was left of her courage. Blanca bolstered it with her vast white calm. "We are passing through, great one," she managed to say: "hunting one of our own. If you would be so kind as to grant us passage . . ."

"Hunting?" the king inquired, purring the word.

"Seeking in order to find," Elen said. Her heart was

beating so hard she could barely hear herself speak. Oh, she was an idiot and a fool for speaking of a hunt before the lord of the Wild Hunt. Someone somewhere on the other side of memory had taught her how one should talk to a Power of Faerie, but all such knowledge had fled under the Horned King's eyeless stare. "The way, it seems, is through your realm."

She held her breath. If she had broken any or all of the many rules and proprieties of Faerie, she might never know it. She would be a spot of blood on the road of bones.

The king forbore to set the hounds upon her. Nor did he laugh at the silly fool of a human. He did not answer, either: not directly. "You are well guarded," he said. "Great power deigns to serve your will." He bowed his crowned head to Blanca and Hera.

"Thank you," Elen said. "We are suitably humbled and awed by the ones who condescend to carry us."

The king bent toward her as if to peer at her face. She did her best not to flinch or shudder. "Tell me," he said. "What prey do you hunt?"

"Nothing worthy of your majesty," Elen said as steadily as she could.

"Indeed?" said the king. "Not perhaps a herd of the Powers, and one as near foaling as one of that kind may be?"

Sara's gasp almost made Elen forget and turn her back on the Horned King—but that, if one valued

one's soul, was most unwise. "How near?" Sara demanded.

"Near," said the king. "Heavy and slow with it. She
paid my toll, did the one who rode with the Powers,
and never blanched at the price."

"What was the price?"

Elen would have hit Sara if she had been close
enough. Was she *trying* to provoke the Horned King?

But the king seemed thoroughly amused. "Every
price is different," he said, "but the substance is the
same: What matters to you most?"

"Did you take one of the mares for your Hunt? Or
the stallion?"

The king laughed, a sound like water flowing beneath a shield of ice. "Why, child of Earth? Should I
have done such a thing?"

"Did you?"

Sara was stubborn. She was also brave beyond belief.
Elen had not understood just how much until now.

"Those are greater Powers than I," said the king. "I
cannot deny that I would be more than glad to welcome
them into the Hunt, but I have no power to compel
them."

"Do you not?"

"I do not," the Horned King said.

Elen had to take back the reins of this conversation before it killed them all. "We will pay to pass," she
said. "Only tell us what you will accept."

The hounds rose from their watchful crouch at the Horned King's feet and loped toward her. They came so fast that she did not even feel the horror of it until afterward. They wove in and out through Blanca's motionless legs, more like cats than dogs, and scrabbled at her feet and legs with their bony paws.

The Horned King raised a leather-gloved hand. The hounds whined in protest but returned obediently to their places. "You have courage," he said.

"I have necessity," Elen said. That was true. Saying it steadied her remarkably. "What will you take? Treasure? One of us?"

"I am not a hoarder of gold," the king said. "Your bones are small and frail, and this city has more than enough of their kind already."

"What price will you take?" Elen asked again.

"What do you value most?" the king answered.

He was talking to Elen, but she knew he meant Sara, too. She hardly had to think about her answer. Apart from her mother and her world, there was one thing. Or person. And Elen was sitting on her.

"She's not mine to give," Elen said.

"He said 'what,'" said Sara, "not 'whom.'"

"My prize from the penning?" Elen said. "But it's not—"

"More than that," Sara said. She was looking at the Horned King as if she understood something that Elen was missing.

What did a person value most? For Elen, it was honesty. Being honest. Telling the truth, even if it hurt. What could a lord of Faerie do with that?

Could she give it up for a Caledonian? Even to save a herd of worldrunners?

"Prove to us that you can open the way," Elen said.

The king bowed. He was mocking her, maybe. Or maybe he thought her rudeness was refreshing.

He came down from the hill until he stood at Blanca's side. She did not react except to tilt an ear. He was not as tall as Elen had thought: as tall as a tall man, certainly, but no giant. She had to look down to see his face.

The light in his right eye socket had grown to fill the orbit of bone.

That was the gate from the worldroad into Caledon. On the other side lay the wasteland and the green valley and the herd of horses. The way ran through the Horned King's eye.

Ria was there. Elen saw her in a stone-walled room. Its one window was open, looking out on the paddock and the mares. She sat on the ledge with her knees drawn up, hugging them tight.

Elen felt strange, looking at her: half furious with hate, and half almost pitying. Ria looked so alone, so lost and so miserable. She did not look happy with herself or her world at all.

"All I have is what I am," Elen said. "My honor; my

lineage. I have a little magic, but it was never trained, and it's not much for use."

"I have all the magic I need," said the Horned King.

"Are you sure?" Elen asked—stupidly, but it was all she could think of.

"Take me," Sara said.

Elen whipped in the saddle—never mind the rules or the danger. "*What?* What are you—"

"I'll stay here," Sara said. Her face was calm and her voice was steady. "I'll do whatever you need me to do. Even—" There, at last, she faltered. "Even if you need me to ride with you."

"Your soul is a bright and shining thing," the Horned King said. In his way, he sounded almost gentle. "But I need no slave or servant. Most certainly I do not need the wrath of the Powers and of those who serve them. No, daughter of the Star, I am neither so brave nor so foolish."

Sara opened her mouth. She looked both angry and frustrated. Elen spoke before she could make matters any worse. "What do you need?"

"Little," the king said, "but of that, very much indeed."

Elen pounded the pommel of the saddle with her fist. The saddle did not shift, and neither did Blanca. "Tell me what you need!"

"That is your bitterest enemy," the Horned King said. "Her world has contested with yours since the

Powers first walked the roads through my realm. Give me that, child of war."

Elen blinked. "Give you—what? My world? A worldrunner? But you said—"

"War," said the king. "Give me your hate and your long mistrust. Give me what breaks worlds and weakens worldroads and scars the substance of Faerie."

Elen went perfectly still. "That's not a price at all!" she wanted to cry. "It's not even possible!" But the words refused to come.

The king's eye darkened. Ria was still inside it. Now she was standing, and Elen could see bruises on her face. Either she had been in a fight, or she had met something on the road that challenged her right to pass.

Her shoulders were back and her chin jutted and she was as haughtily defiant as any Caledonian could be. But Elen saw fear in her eyes—not for herself but for the mares outside her window. One in particular was so big with foal that her belly seemed almost to drag the ground.

There was sweat on her neck. Her haunches were sunken and her tail seemed oddly limp. When she shifted her uncomfortable weight, milk spurted from the swollen udder.

Elen knew the signs. The mare was ready to foal. And Elen and Sara were trapped here, helpless to do anything.

"I can't make peace for both worlds," Elen said in despair. "I can't even do it for myself."

"You have more power than you know," the king said.

"*What* power? I'm just a fool of a girl!"

"A girl who loves horses," the king said.

In its eye was another, at least as much a fool, who loved horses just as much. She had done something beyond forgiveness, but maybe there was still time to undo it.

"You want me to stop hating Caledon," Elen said.

"One Caledonian will do," the king said.

That was a trick and a trap, and Elen would not be surprised in the least if John David had something to do with it. Somehow. With the powers that he had, and the Powers he served—of which the Horned King might well be one. Or did John David and the Horned King both, in their separate ways, serve something greater than they?

A mare was going to foal away from Earth, where it was deadly for her kind to foal. The baby, a world-runner, a Power among the worlds, would die.

"I'll do it for the horses," Elen said. "That's the only reason. If it's not enough . . ."

"It will do," the Horned King said.

"Promise us something," said Elen. She felt Blanca's approval. This was right, Blanca let her know. It was also wise. "Promise you won't hunt us when we try to get back to Earth again."

"You have my word," said the Horned King.

Elen drew in a sharp breath. "There is one more thing." The king waited; she could not tell if he was angry or impatient or insulted. He simply stood beside Blanca, staring at her with one eyeless socket full of darkness and the other full of a farmstead in Caledon. "If we need you out there, can we call on you? Will you help us?"

She hardly knew where that came from. Old stories, partly. When bargaining with Faerie, the wise mortal got as much from the exchange as she could. And part of it was Blanca. Blanca wanted her to do this.

The Horned King spoke to Blanca and not to Elen. "If the Powers need me, I will come."

Blanca turned her head to look at him. He bowed low, even to the ground. "So let it be," he said.

Elen waited to feel something—the jolt of a spell, the inward twisting of an incantation—but she felt just the same. She still hated Caledon. She still knew she had to save the mares, and get Ria out of there, and get them all back to Rancho Estrella to face the accounting.

She knew nothing better to say than, "I'm ready."

The Horned King rose up from the ground—rose and rose and rose, until he towered to the sky. He lowered his head then until the gate of his skull opened directly in front of Blanca.

Elen had been through ice and fire, and had traveled on a shaft of sun. This could send her straight to her soul's destruction, with Blanca and Hera and Sara following—because they trusted her.

Trust was all the world to a horse and a rider. Elen recognized it for the great gift that it was.

She gave it to the Horned King, in spite of everything she had heard about the treachery of Faerie. She rode Blanca through the gate of bone.

CHAPTER 17

It felt like walking through mist and ice and fog, and smelled like the breath of graves. Any instant Elen was sure the gate would clash shut upon them and they would all be gone.

The worldrunners carried them through the mist and the fog into a forest of tall trees, in air so cool it felt cold. Its smell was more than wonderful.

"Caledon," Elen said, as much to hear herself say it as to let Sara know where they were. She tried not to put such a twist of loathing in it—because after all that had been the price she paid to come here.

There was no doubt that it was Caledon. Those trees only grew there, evergreen, stretching up to the lowering sky. Cascades of cream-white flowers bloomed on the branches, breathing out that heavenly fragrance. She closed her eyes and breathed it in. No one had told her there was such beauty in this world.

Blanca's teeth clinked against the bit. Behind her Sara said something indistinct: talking to Hera. Both mares were fretting, looking ahead through the trees.

Elen let Blanca stride forward, moving into a trot. Hera pressed close behind. Sara had gone quiet again, but her presence was strong at Elen's back. Whatever Elen needed of her, Elen would have.

The trees gave way to grassy emptiness. Down the rolling hill, the wall and the roofs of the farmstead stood out distinct in the grey light.

Blanca stopped short. Elen nearly went over her head. There was no wall for her to run into, no barrier that Elen could see, but Blanca could not go forward at all. Nor could Hera.

Elen slipped off Blanca's back, stretching out her hand. It met no barrier, visible or otherwise. She felt something as she stepped from the wood into the field, a tugging at her insides, and a slight but notice-able itch. It was nothing to stop her; it merely told her that there was a spell at work, drawing from what little was in the earth and air of Caledon.

She turned back toward the mares. Sara stood beside them, no more able to pass than they were. "How are you doing that?"

"I'm not from Earth," Elen said. "Or I'm not a worldrunner or her rider. Or both."

"And you're part Caledonian."

Elen stiffened. She bit down hard on the first response, the snap of anger. She said instead, "Maybe that's it. It's clearly set to bar hunters from Earth, and worldrunners."

"That's not good," said Sara. "If we can't get in, that means the mares can't get out."

"Maybe," said Elen. "I can go in—they didn't set the trap for me."

"Are you sure?"

Elen was not, at all. But she was not about to let Sara know that. "Don't worry. I'll be safe."

"You can't go alone."

"I'll have to, won't I?"

Sara had no answer for that.

"Look," Elen said. "Once I'm in, I'll see if I can get the mares to open a worldroad and escape. Then we can take care of Ria."

"Somebody will have to ride at least one of the mares," Sara said.

"But—" Elen began. Blanca moved as if at random, coming between the two of them. Elen stared at the white wall of her shoulder.

So. It was a secret that Blanca did not always need a rider to direct her.

John David knew. Other worldriders must.

John David was not there. Sara was. And Blanca wanted Elen to keep it to herself.

"Can you break down the barrier?" Sara asked from the far side of Blanca. "Is there a way to do that?"

"Not without setting off every alarm in the world," Elen said.

"Just go in, then," Sara said. "See how many guards there are. Watch and spy, then come back here. *Don't* get caught."

Elen bristled, but bit down the quick retort. Sara made sense, as far as she went. "You go back on the road," Elen said. "Wait for us. We'll be there as soon as we can."

"I can't just abandon you," Sara said.

"You're not going to. You're going to focus on getting back to Earth," Elen said as patiently as she could. "Keep that in your mind when you get on the road, but stay. Wait for us."

Sara's chin set. She was shutting down, refusing to see anything but Elen alone among her worst enemies. Elen pushed as hard as she dared. "We need you to mark the way. We'll aim for you. As soon as we get there, be prepared to run."

That got through. Not easily, and Sara was not willing, but finally she gave in. "Be careful," she said.

As angry and worried and frustrated as she was, it sounded like an accusation.

Elen heard the spirit and not the tone. "I'll meet you soon. Be ready when we come."

"As ready as I can be," Sara said.

She had committed to it. Elen eyed her warily, but the only choice was to trust her.

Maybe that was part of the Horned King's price, too. It was such a simple thing, and so very difficult.

Elen hugged her quickly—braced for her to recoil, and somewhat startled when she hugged back. They hesitated for a dragging instant, groping for words.

There were none that would be enough. Elen nodded stiffly; so did Sara. Elen turned away, toward the field and the house of her enemies.

She pushed fear down deep and locked it in. She focused on crossing the open space without being caught, and on getting over the wall.

She crouched down low and glided through the tall grass. Nothing living stirred, not even a bird in the air. There was no guard visible on the wall.

Maybe Ria was there alone with the horses.

That made no sense. There had to be others in the farmstead. They would be trusting to their barrier, and expecting nothing of their own world to cross the wasteland that surrounded their green valley.

Elen stopped at the foot of the wall. It was half again as tall as she was, made of mortared stone, and it looked new. There was no gate on this side.

She eyed possible handholds and pondered the wisdom of trying the gate, if she could find one. Caledonians would be crazy enough to build a wall without one, and brick up worldrunners inside it—as if a worldrunner could not find a worldroad wherever she was.

There was a gate after all, down past the corner, facing the lake. A track led from it to the shore. The water was perfectly still, though a faint wind stirred the tendrils of hair that had escaped Elen's braid.

The gate was made of wood bound with iron. Her fingers stung faintly as she ran them over the surface, but the spell was nearly worn away. Whoever had laid it had not built it to last.

This was not the might of Caledon that she had been taught to hate and fear. What she saw, here and from the worldroad, was a broken world, its tide of magic so low it barely existed at all, and its people desperate to find a way, any way, to keep their world alive.

It was hard to see that, and harder to realize that Ymbria, though damaged, was in much better state than Caledon. Part of her exulted—finally, the war would end, and Caledon would be dead—but it was a rapidly shrinking part. The rest remembered that there were people here, people who lived and breathed and felt joy and pain just as she did. If their world died, so would they.

Her cheeks were wet, and not with rain. She struck the door with her fist. To her amazement, it gave way.

This was a small door, a back door like the one that led to the hidden half of Rancho Estrella. She looked, blinking, at the back of a barn, and a narrow yard overgrown with grass and weeds.

The steading must have been a horse farm once. The barn was bigger than the main barn on the ranch and could have held twice as many horses, but it looked shabby and neglected. She would have said it was deserted, but then she heard voices talking.

She pushed herself up off her bruised knees, shut the door carefully behind her, and tiptoed to the nearest window. The voices were some distance away, but when she pressed her ear to the shutter, she could make out most of the words.

Two men were talking: a deep voice and one that sounded lighter and younger. The deep one spoke first.

"Do you believe her?"

"I believe she thinks it's true. So do the rest of the worlds."

"A mare's a mare," the older man said. "I've foaled

out hundreds, and this one looks like any of her sisters. She's not even bothered by the change of worlds."

"My sister says she is. She's just too brave to show it."

"Your sister," the older man said in a tone that made Elen think he wanted to spit, "is a bleeding heart for horses. We should have sent you after all. You could at least have won over the Ymbrian with your pretty face—and not gone all weak-kneed at the thought of hurting a horse."

"I don't want to hurt her, either," the boy said with a touch of heat. "Nor should you."

"Sometimes you have to hurt to help."

If the boy had an answer for that, it was not in words.

Elen pressed against the chill stone wall. For the first time she was cold in her light shirt and jacket. The boy sounded more or less reasonable, but the man sounded like the kind of Caledonian she had been taught to hate.

As she stood listening, finding nothing inside now but silence, a thin, cold rain began to fall. She edged away from the window, flitting down along the barn wall and edging around the corner. The space opened up there, a rectangle of sand marked out for a riding arena, with the barn she hid behind on one long side. Another barn marked one of the short ends. The farmhouse and its buildings clustered on the far side.

196 ★ CAITLIN BRENNAN

The mares were in the paddock on the second short side, with an open barn for shelter. They were all heavily pregnant. The heaviest, a flaxen-maned chestnut, stood away from the others, out in the rain.

The man and the boy leaned on the fence under the overhang of the roof. The man was big and broad-shouldered, with a greying red-brown beard. The boy did not look like Ria at all, except for his height. He could have been one of Elen's own brothers, with his black curly hair and his smooth brown skin.

Caledon had Ymbrian blood in its princes, too. In Ymbria, a boy who looked as much like the enemy as this one did would have to fight for every scrap of respect or trust. His face would have shown it, and the way he carried himself.

There was no sign of that here. "Tonight, you think?" he asked the older man.

The man shrugged. "No way to tell with mares. My guess? Tomorrow night at the latest."

"We'd better get her under cover, then," the boy said.

"In a while," said the man. "Let's get some rest. We'll be up all night with her, whether or not she drops the foal."

The boy looked as if he might object, but the rain closed in hard, and the mare moved slowly and heavily into the far corner of the barn. Then the boy would leave her.

Ria was not the only horse person in that family,

Elen could see. She waited for the boy and the man to disappear into the largest of the farm buildings before she ventured along the edge of the arena.

She braced for the mares to betray her, but although the chestnut with the crooked blaze turned briefly to look at her, the rest ignored her. They had hay and shelter, and the rain was getting heavier. That was all they needed to know in this world.

CHAPTER 18

Elen found Ria much sooner than she had feared, but it was not going to be as easy to get her out of there as Elen had hoped. Such plan as Elen had had, to catch her alone and convince her to help Elen get the mares back to Earth before they foaled, fell apart before the fact that Ria was anything but alone, and she seemed perfectly comfortable.

She was in the big stone-floored kitchen of the farmhouse, and there were four men with her: the man and the boy whom Elen had already seen, and a pair of tall redheads who were, from what they said while Elen listened, Ria's cousins.

It was small for a conspiracy, but it had been enough to steal four worldrunners. The two redheaded men were making dinner: baking bread, stirring pots. Ria sat on a stool at the tall stone-topped table, chin on fists. There was a shallow bowl in front of her, and light gleamed from it.

She was scrying as she had in the fountain under the ramada. Her brother bent to see what she was looking at. Then Elen could see they had the same nose and chin. "Still the same old draggy-bellied mare," he said.

"Mares like to surprise you," said Ria.

Elen slipped in behind the boy and the man and made herself one of the shadows in the corner past the wide stone hearth. She worked hard to keep her heart from pounding and her breath from coming so quick and hard they all heard it. But worse than that was her stomach, which wanted desperately to growl. She had last eaten worlds ago, and the Caledonians' dinner smelled wonderful.

They took forever to eat it and clean up after it. The men went to bed after that. Ria stayed by the scrying bowl. Her family mocked her for it, but she ignored them.

After they were gone, her whole expression changed, face and body both. All her ease evaporated; she drew up tight. She pushed herself away from the table and spun around the room, and let out a wordless sound, half growl and half groan. "Oh, dear gods, I hope he is right and I am wrong, and that is just a mare and the rest is a myth to keep the worlds from breeding their own."

"It's not a myth," Elen said.

Ria stopped short.

"It's true," said Elen. "We can't let that mare foal here. It will come out all wrong. She'll die."

Ria peered into the shadows. "What in the name of . . . ?"

Elen stepped out into the light. She would not swear to it, but she almost thought she saw relief in Ria's face, before it went stiff and hostile.

"How did you get here?" Ria demanded. "What spell did you use? How did you get through the wall?"

"I walked," Elen said. "I'm good at hiding."

"Except when you're not," Ria said. "If my uncle or my cousins catch you, they won't even bother to hold you for ransom."

"And your brother?" Elen asked.

"Emrys might apologize before he kills you." Ria sat back down at the table and bent once more over the bowl. "There are stupider things you could have done, but offhand I can't think of any. Who sent you to spy on us? John David?"

"No," Elen said. She resisted the temptation to tell Ria where Sara and the worldrunners were. This might be a trap, or at least there must be someone spying, from the way Ria was acting.

Ria seemed surprised at her answer. "You came by yourself? That's not just stupid, it's crazy."

"So is laying wards that keep anything of Earth out, but not someone like me. Someone with Caledonian blood."

"That was the boys being arrogant," Ria said, "and me not bothering to argue."

"You *wanted* to trap me?" Elen's voice was rising. She fought to keep it quiet, and to push down the swelling of rage. She had to stop that. She had given her word. She had to look at Ria as part of the tribe, her tribe, not as the enemy. No matter how hard it was.

Ria's flat stare did not help at all. Elen made herself say what she would have said to someone from Ymbria—or to Sara. "You wanted me to find you. To help you get the mares out."

"That was crazy of me, wasn't it?"

"Not as crazy as me actually doing it." Elen paused. She should not say it, but she had to. "And yet you brought them here. How am I supposed to get past that?"

"I swore an oath," Ria said. "I don't know if you can understand. When I did it, I hadn't seen the ranch yet, or met anybody there. I just knew what we had to do to survive. I didn't realize everything that it would mean."

"Neither did I," Elen said, very low. Then, louder: "I think I know how to do it. I'll need your help."

"You're actually admitting it?"

"I am admitting it," Elen said.

"Well, then," said Ria, "I'll do what I can."

There was a silence. They stared at each other. Elen could feel the hate trying to take its old place inside her. But she had bound herself to change. For the worldrunners. To save the baby that was so close to being born.

"Tell me where Moondance is," she said.

Ria's hands clenched into fists on the table. "I don't know. I got off on the road, where there was a stream. He bolted. I managed to hold on to the mares, but he was gone."

Elen's heart had knotted as tight as Ria's fists. "Maybe he went home," she said. "It doesn't matter anyway. Not just now. Can you make sure everybody here stays asleep for the next hour? Or longer if possible?"

"I can do that," Ria said a little slowly, but confidently enough. "I know a spell. If your Ymbrian delicacy can stand the thought of it."

Elen bit back a sharp retort. "Do it," she said, "and wait. I'll be back."

"Where will you—"

"Just wait," said Elen.

Maybe she should have trusted Ria more, and told her where Sara and the worldrunners were. But

Elen's gut told her not to do it. The less Ria knew, the less anyone could get out of her.

It was easier to get out of the farmstead than it had been to get in. Elen felt the sleep spell spreading even before she reached the wall. It tangled her feet and nearly brought her down, but she fought free of it.

She had to fight free of other things, too—including a completely unexpected surge of envy. Elen had never been allowed to learn magic. She was too young, and magic was too powerful a thing to trust to a child.

Caledon was different. Not better or worse. Simply different.

Sara was not where Elen had left her. Before Elen could panic, a snort from deeper in the wood led her to Blanca. Hera was grazing with her in a clearing. Sara had made a shelter of branches and settled under it with the saddles.

She was glad to share the bread and cheese that Elen had brought from the farm. There was no time to linger over it, but they needed all the strength they could scrape together.

When they had both eaten as much as they could choke down, Elen pulled the medallion out of her pocket. It looked almost like gold in the grey light of

Caledon, and the star on its face seemed to shimmer. "Take this," she said to Sara. "It's part of me now. Wherever it goes, I'll be able to find it."

"Oh, no," said Sara. "We're not splitting up again."

"We have to," Elen said. "You have to go ahead. Blanca will take you to a safe place. I'll get the mares out and find you."

"Blanca will take me?" Sara repeated. "How can she—"

"She can," Elen said. She was not as sure of it as she tried to sound. Blanca was grazing like any ordinary horse, shaking her ears and blowing at a fly.

She raised her head. Her deep wise eye looked into Elen's. Yes, she would do it. She knew a place; she would take Sara there.

Someone else moved behind Blanca: big square head, steel-grey body. It was Moondance. Blanca's nostrils fluttered a greeting. He rumbled at her, arching his neck. She flattened ears in warning. None of his stallion nonsense now. They had work to do.

Elen had not seen Moondance come into the clearing, and yet there he was, with no sign on him of where he had been or what he had been doing. He was wearing a bridle but no saddle.

She had had a plan, such as it was. At sight of Moondance, she knew how to make it work.

"If you will," she said to him.

He was not inside her the way Blanca was, but for

once he acknowledged her existence: he tossed his head and stamped. She took that for a yes.

Everything she did on this adventure was a test of trust. It was humbling, and so annoying it made her skin twitch.

"Try not to get killed," Sara said.

"You, too," said Elen.

They hung on that, needing to go but unable to move.

Elen pulled away first. Or maybe it was Sara. Blanca led her down the straight track in the wood. Elen took hold of Moondance's reins.

She was risking it all on a glimmer of trust, gambling on a hope and a guess. She led him toward the field.

He felt the barrier: he checked and jibbed. But when Elen coaxed him forward, he came—mincing, shying, but able to step out into the tall grass.

Elen had guessed right. He was included in the Caledonians' warding spell, even if he had not been there when it was made. He could come inside it.

He did not like the way it felt, at all. His ears went from flat to tensely pricked and back again, and he hunched his back and tucked his tail. When Elen laid a hand on his neck, he squealed and struck, nearly catching her with his hoof.

She slapped him for that. Her small hand hardly even stung his heavy neck, but the sound caught his attention. He settled down, more or less: his eyes were white-rimmed and his nostrils were flared as wide as they would go.

There was no creeping up on the farmstead with a restless, barely controllable stallion. Elen had to submit herself to more trust, this time of Ria and her spellcasting, and lead Moondance boldly up to the gate.

It opened easily, with no lingering tingle of protection. Everything was quiet inside. The sleep spell lapped like waves at the inner wall.

The mares were awake in their paddock. Moondance called to them in a voice that should have roused the dead. They raised their heads and whickered back.

Elen's heart was beating so hard she was dizzy. It was all she could do to hold onto Moondance and keep from getting kicked or trampled.

He reared and twisted and broke free. Elen staggered and almost fell. Moondance bolted toward the mares.

It was all falling apart, and it had barely begun. Elen wobbled between the paddock and the house. If Moondance took the mares and ran for the worldroad, she would be stranded here. But if she ran after him, she would lose Ria.

This was Ria's world. She was safe here.

That was not what Elen had determined to do. The mares had to go back to Earth, and so did Ria.

They all had to go together. Then Ria would face the consequences for what she did.

Elen groaned. "*Wait* for us!" she called out to Moondance. There was no way to tell if he understood her, or if he even wanted to. His tiny little stallion mind was focused on his mares. She spun and ran toward the house.

The door flew open. Ria nearly crashed into Elen on the path. She was babbling so rapidly that Elen could hardly understand her. "He's in my head. How did he get in my head? He's screaming at me. The baby's coming, the baby's coming. It can't be born here. He won't stop saying it. He has to get his mare away. He has to take her *now!*"

"Yes, he does!" Elen cried, drowning Ria out. "But he has to take us, too. Make him listen. Make him wait just a little longer."

That got through Ria's wall of words. She bolted for the paddock.

The spell's tide had started to ebb. Any moment now, the Caledonians would wake—and they would not be happy. Not in the slightest. Elen ran faster.

Moondance was in no mood to be obedient. He was the stallion. The stallion defended the herd. He had to defend his herd.

Ria kept trying to catch hold of his flying reins, and never mind the flying hooves that could crush her skull in an instant. "Forget the bridle!" Elen yelled at her. "Try to get into his head!"

She had no way to tell if Ria understood, and no time to find out. Moondance's high dramatics had all the mares in a lather, but the chestnut who was closest to foaling was too heavy and slow to do more than trot along the fence.

Elen had spotted a halter and lead hung on a rail just as it would be at the ranch. It was a halter from Earth, its bright green faded by a hotter sun than had ever shone here.

She got it on the mare and got to her stop, took her head in both hands and pressed her forehead to the mare's and said, "Please. We need to get you to a safe place."

The mare stood still. She sighed.

"Make a road for us," Elen said.

The mare was not Blanca. If she understood Elen, she did not show it. Her eyes focused inward; her ears twitched back, going briefly flat.

The baby was trying to come into this alien world that would twist and rend it as soon as it left its mother's body. She was holding it in. No mare, no matter how determined she was, could do that forever.

The other mares were not much help. They were all focused on the same thing: on keeping their babies from being born. Elen desperately needed Blanca, with her calm and her good sense and her mastery of the roads. The best that Elen had in that place was Moondance—and he had the same attachment to Ria that Blanca did to Elen.

Probably there was a name for it, some high and hidden word that only worldriders knew. Whatever it was, they needed it now, badly. People were stirring in the house. A man's voice called out faintly.

Maybe he was dreaming. Elen dragged the haltered mare toward Moondance, who had finally stopped acting like an idiot.

Ria had the reins again. She was flushed, and from the way she moved, she had caught at least one kick. But she was not bleeding, and there seemed to be nothing broken.

"Make him listen to you," Elen said. "We've got to get out of here."

Ria's face locked shut. She shook her head. "I can't go. Take him, quick. I'll get the gate open."

"You don't have a choice," Elen said.

"I have to stay. I'll keep anyone from following for as long as I can."

"They can't follow us on the worldroads," Elen said.

"Can't they?"

"It's not wise to try it without a worldrunner. And we have all of those that they're getting their hands on."

"My people are long past wisdom," Ria said.

There was no arguing the truth of that. "Get on and ride," Elen said. "Tell him to find Blanca."

Ria was not going to do as she was told. Moondance did not look likely to help, either. Elen looked up beyond him to see a face in the window of the house: narrow, brown, and startled.

CHAPTER 19

Elen knotted the mare's lead around her neck and sprinted for the gate. Moondance reared just beyond it, with precious little help or hindrance from Ria.

Elen was not even thinking by then. She seized Ria bodily and flung her toward the stallion.

When Ria staggered against him, he dropped his shoulder and turned his body just so. She had to grab mane or fall under him; when they both stopped moving, she was on his back and the mares were trotting through the opened gate.

The chestnut was not the last to escape. That was an elegant little bay with one white foot. She was not quite so heavy with foal as the rest; as she passed, Elen ran with her until the force of their combined movement let her swing astride.

Elen had ridden bareback and bridleless when she was much younger, but never on a completely strange horse. It was exhilarating and terrifying and absolutely necessary.

The mares moved together in a line behind Moondance, and their line was perfectly straight. They aimed directly across the arena, toward the house with Ria's brother still standing motionless in the window under the eaves.

That sank in as the clouds parted. The boy had not moved to call his kinsmen. He was watching silently, with no expression.

He saw them, Elen was sure: he looked straight into her eyes. He said nothing, did nothing. He simply let them go.

The sun's angle was low; a shaft of light slanted down onto the sand. Moondance ascended as if it had been a solid road, and the mares followed.

As the whitefoot bay left the sand for the road of light, a shout rang out behind. It was a deeper voice than the boy's, older and harsher. The uncle ran out of the house. He had a crossbow, and he aimed it at Moondance.

The bolt flew true. Ria cried out, sharp and fierce, and slapped it aside.

A rain of bolts followed, but by luck or the power of the road, none found a target.

The sun was fading fast. The clouds were closing in. Moondance quickened to a canter. The mares lumbered as best they could in his wake.

One by one they cantered out of the world. Little by little the road shrank and faded. In the moment before it vanished, the bay mare plunged into the cold mist of cloud.

Almost too late Elen remembered to fix her mind on the images on the medallion: the mountain and the star. Where they were was Blanca. Where Blanca was, was safety.

She held to that with all the strength she had. The cloud wrapped around her. She could just see the rump and tail of the mare in front of her. She had to trust—that again, by the gods—that the rest were still ahead, and Ria on Moondance leading them all.

Blanca. Mountain. Star. Safety; a place where a worldrunner could be born.

Inside the cloud, riding a mare who carried a worldrunner foal, Elen let urgency sharpen her focus. She could feel Blanca inside her head, big and white and quiet. She followed that feeling down into the center of her heart.

The cloud evaporated around Elen. Light blinded her: sun shining in a fiercely blue sky. She saw the mares ahead of her on the road of light, and Moondance in the lead where he should be.

Sharp-toothed red-brown mountains reared up on all sides. A canyon opened below. Its rock walls were sheer; its bottom was green with trees and grass. A river ran through it.

Ria whooped. "We did it! We made it to Earth!"

"We *didn't*!" Elen shouted back. "It's not Earth. It's an outland of Faerie. You're the one with the magic. Can't you feel it?"

Ria's stricken expression told Elen she could. "We can't stay here. We've got to keep going."

"Blanca says it's safe," Elen said.

"But," said Ria, "how can it be? After all the panic and the screaming, this isn't Earth, either."

Blanca's answer was too far and vague to make much sense. *Safe*, was the most Elen could gain from it. *Come.*

The straight track touched ground just short of the canyon's edge. From there it was not a worldroad any more: it wound down into the deep cut, twisting back and forth upon itself, all the way to the river on the bottom.

In the region of Earth where the ranch was, the realm called Arizona, the farther downhill one went, the hotter it was. Heights were as cool as anything ever got. Lowlands were burning hells.

Faerie was different. It was cool down in the canyon, and the sun felt softer. Elen breathed in the damp green smell. It was still a desert smell, with dust in it, and a nose-tickling undertone like Earth's greasewood and sage, but the sharp edge was blunted.

The trail wound to an end beside the river. The stream was wide and shallow, winding through thickets of cottonwoods. Birds sang and chattered in the trees, and something small and brown and quick darted away under a log.

"This is odd," Elen said.

Ria glanced at her. "What?"

"There's nothing living up above," said Elen. "Not a bird, not even a lizard. But look at all the creatures here."

Ria nodded. "They're all harmless. Look: no snakes or scorpions. The horses aren't finding anything at all to shy at."

"It's safe," Elen said. "That's what Blanca means."

"Safe for a worldrunner to foal in?"

"I don't know," said Elen with a touch of temper. "All I know is what she's telling me."

Ria's brows had drawn together, but she spared Elen any more of her questions.

The horses left the bank and waded into the river, lowered their heads and drank. At its deepest it only came up to their knees.

If it was safe for them, Elen had to believe it was safe for humans. She slid off into water so cold she gasped with the shock.

It tasted like the sky. It filled her like the best and biggest breakfast she ever ate. When she stood up straight and simply breathed, she saw that Ria was sliding down off Moondance's back, keeping a firm grip on his reins.

Elen waited while she drank. It seemed to take forever, but it must have only been a handful of heartbeats. Finally, when Ria lifted her head, Elen said, "We need to move on. There's a safe place ahead, but I don't think we have much time."

Ria followed her stare to the most pregnant of the mares. There was sweat on the sleek red neck, and the massive belly had almost disappeared.

"That's not good," Ria said.

"No," said Elen. "The baby's in place. It's ready to be born. We've got to find Blanca and the others and get to Earth. The sooner the better."

They found a trail on the other side of the river, running along the bank, wide and high enough for horses.

Elen kept glancing over her shoulder, expecting the road to disappear, but it stayed open behind her.

The trail was too twisty to see farther than a handful of horse-lengths ahead, but the footing was firm sand, and it sloped upward a little. If Elen had known where it went, she would have loved riding on it: it was wonderful footing to trot and canter on.

They stayed in a walk. The sorrel mare was moving slowly now, and Elen did not like the way her neck and shoulders were dark with sweat. None of the other horses was sweating at all.

The sun had sunk almost to the canyon walls when the track bent through a narrow band of trees into a green field. The grass looked as if it had grown there that morning, it was so bright and new.

"Look!" Ria said. She was riding ahead; she raised her arm and pointed.

At the far end of the field was a low stone house. A corral stood next to it, with a fence made of weathered rails.

Blanca and Hera stood in the corral, heads up, ears up, watching the newcomers come closer. Elen felt Blanca's call in her bones, a clear and imperious summons. *Come here! Come now! All of you!*

Sara came around the house with a pair of leather buckets. Her eyes went wide; she dropped the buckets and ran to throw the gate open and let the mares in.

Moondance tried to get in, too, but Ria held him

back. "Come on down here," Sara said. She led them to a smaller corral down past the end of the large one, with its own bit of shelter, and water in a barrel, and grass to graze on.

He stopped fussing once his bridle was off and he had had a long roll and settled to cropping grass. Sara and Ria left him there and came back to Elen, who was still standing by the gate into the mares' paddock. The shadows in it were dark and long.

"We really shouldn't stay here," Ria said. "The sorrel looks awfully close to foaling, and it's almost sunset."

"Blanca says it's safe," said Elen.

"How can it be safe?" Ria said. "This isn't Earth."

It is safe, Blanca repeated. *We make it safe. Come!*

Elen stayed where she was. "Great Powers," she said, remembering the Horned King's words, "above even a lord of Faerie. What are you really?"

Blanca, the mare answered.

Elen felt the turning of her mind away from matters that she considered unimportant, toward the one thing that mattered. Her whole body pointed toward the corner of the corral.

CHAPTER 20

The red mare was pacing and lashing her tail. The other mares stood back to give her room. As Elen stared, she folded her forelegs and dropped her front end. Her hind was slower; as it went down, water gushed.

The mare was having her baby. Right here. Right now.

"She can't do that," Elen said stupidly.

"Her name is Grace," Ria said.

"So," Elen said without even thinking. "You care what you steal."

Ria shot her a withering look. Elen braced for the

lash of words, but Ria's eyes had snapped back to the corral.

A white bubble swelled under Grace's tail. That was the sac. There should be feet inside it, one behind the other. Then the nose. Then the head and knees. Then the difficult part: the shoulders and elbows. And then the rest should come out in a smooth long slide.

Elen knew all that. She had seen it in her own world, and helped with it, too. But not a worldrunner. Not in Faerie.

"Should we go in?" Ria asked.

She was talking to Sara, who shook her head. "Let her do her business. We can't stop it now."

"There's no way we can even try?"

"No," Sara said. "Not now the water's broken. She has to get the baby out as fast as she can, or the baby will die."

"The baby will die anyway," said Ria. She sounded ready to cry. "This isn't Earth."

We make it Earth, Blanca said.

Elen heard the words. So, to her surprise as much as theirs, did Ria and Sara: they turned to stare at Blanca.

Where we are, Blanca said, *is Earth.*

Ria tossed her hair out of her face. "Is it now? Then why didn't we stay in Caledon?"

It is Caledon, Blanca said.

Elen would have seized on that once, but she had a

promise to the Horned King to keep. She took time to look below the words, to feel what Blanca was feeling. "Caledon is a world, a fixed place that is not Earth. This is part of Faerie. It can be whatever a Power needs it to be."

"Even a foaling place?"

"If it has to be."

"That," said Sara, "is going to upset so many people in so many different ways, it might even make them think your war isn't so bad."

"Especially since the war made it happen in the first place." Suddenly Elen was massively, cripplingly tired. She leaned against the fence and closed her eyes for a moment, but she opened them quickly and shook herself. She could not afford to fall asleep now.

The sun touched the top of the canyon. The air was cooling down quickly, even more quickly than the foal's feet started to appear.

They had nothing to help Grace but their hands and what knowledge any of them had. They did not even have a light.

"Can you make one?" she asked Ria.

Ria shook her head. Her eyes were a little too wide. "Not in Faerie. Using magic here is the most dangerous thing you can do. You can call down things that make the Hunt look like fluffy kittens."

"Even if the worldrunners have decided this part of Faerie is Earth?"

"I don't dare," Ria said.

It was getting darker by the instant. They had to be able to see. Elen wasted no time cursing Ria's cowardice. She said calmly and quietly to the air around Grace, "Please, we need light. Can you keep some of the sun's brightness around her, if you don't mind?"

For a long stretch of breaths she was sure it was useless. Worse, it was silly: asking nothing in particular to do something impossible.

Then she realized something had happened. The soft, rose-gold glow of sunset grew brighter around Grace as the shadows grew darker.

"Thank you," Elen said, and bowed to whatever spirit of goodwill had given the gift.

When she looked up, she saw blue sky still above the canyon's rim, though it was as dark as night below. Up above them, what had been empty space was full of shadowy shapes on things that were not exactly horses, and skeleton dogs, and a tall king with a crown of antlers.

The Wild Hunt had found them.

Elen shivered with cold that had nothing to do with the swiftly cooling air. "They can't be hunting us," she said to herself. "They promised."

As long as they stayed where they were, Elen convinced herself to forget about them. She had other and more pressing things to worry about.

As fast as a foaling needed to be, it was not instant.

There was time for night to fall, and for the dark to come down. The stars shone hard and bright in the pitch-black sky. The shadowy Hunt was still lined up along the top of the canyon, unmoving, as if it was carved out of stone.

The others said nothing about the watchers. Elen wondered if she was the only one who could see. Maybe she was imagining them. Maybe they were not there at all.

Ria's voice broke into her mental babbling. "Is it supposed to take this long for the baby to come out?"

"No," Sara said. "I don't think so. Though maybe—"

Elen was not going to waste time with words. She slipped through the rails of the corral.

Grace lay flat on her side, legs out stiffly, groaning and straining. Both of the foal's legs were out to the knees, but there was no blunt curve of the nose.

That was not good. Elen's sight focused narrowly, the way it did when she wanted to panic but needed to be very, very calm. She pushed up her sleeve and reached inside, along the knobbly wet length of the legs.

It was warm in there, and wet, and slippery. Powerful muscles squeezed her arm; she stopped and waited, barely breathing, until the spasm passed. Then she went in farther.

The word that came was in Ymbrian, and it was not a polite word at all.

"What!" Ria yelled at her.

She found the English to yell back: "I can't find the nose!"

"Well, find it!"

She flamed the Caledonian with her glare, but even while she did that, she shifted and strained to give herself a longer reach. It was not the easiest thing she had ever done, with Grace's contractions trying to push her back out, and having to be so careful not to break or tear anything inside—most of all the membrane the foal was in. If she did that, the baby would suffocate.

Then she found something. Her fingers traced the shape. "The head is turned back," she said. Her voice was perfectly flat. "That's the worst way. There's no way—"

"There had better be," Ria said.

"This is your fault!" Elen flared at her. "If you hadn't stolen her—"

She broke off. Ria looked as stricken as she could have wished. But she had made a promise. As hard as it was, she made herself say, "All right. Maybe it isn't. Foals die on Earth, too. Not," she said, "that I intend to let that happen."

She let another contraction push her arm out, and turned her eyes to Sara. "Do you know of anything we can do? We've got to do something, or they'll both die."

Sara's face had no color in it at all. "We'll have to

cut," she said. "There are knives in the cabin that we can use to cut the foal apart. Then we can get it out."

Elen's stomach clamped tight. She was dangerously close to throwing up. "*No!* That's worse than nothing."

"Nothing is worse," Ria said. "If we get the baby out, maybe we can save Grace."

"Maybe," Sara said. She sounded as sick as Elen felt. "I'll get the knives."

"No," Elen said again. She took her jacket off and wiped her arm dry. Sara was turning already, and Ria was standing there, ready to help with this horrible thing.

Elen looked down at Grace, who was still trying to give birth to a baby who could not move, not the way it was twisted inside. Then her eyes flashed up past the circle of light to the canyon's rim, to the shapes that were still there, still waiting, just visible in starlight. The idea that came to her was completely and perfectly insane.

But then, she thought, why not? What did she have to lose that was worth more than this foal?

She raised her voice so that anything that listened could hear. "Great one! Listen. I'm trying to keep my promise. Can you keep yours? We need help."

Ria and Sara both exploded at once.

"What are you doing?"

"Have you gone straight screaming out of your mind?"

She ignored them. That baby was not going to die, and neither was its mother.

For a terribly long while after her half-scream, the night was perfectly silent. Even Grace had stopped straining. Then Elen heard the soft sound of wings and the rattle of bones, and a sound like ghostly bells.

The Wild Hunt came down like a snowfall, drifting to the ground all around them. They brought a chill that felt lovely in the hot night, and dimmed the light around Grace so far that Elen squawked. "No! We need to see."

The light came back to most of what it had been before. Elen looked past Sara's wide, shocked stare and Ria's complete stillness to the two Hunters who were closest. One was a skeleton in tarnished silver armor, and the other was the Horned King.

He came to the edge of the light. He was different than he had been in the city of bones: no longer a skeleton in rags of leather and cloth, but a figure like a man, tall and strong and very much alive. At first Elen thought the antlers grew out of his head, but now that he was close enough, she saw that it was a headdress made of an elk's head and neck. The face and eyes beneath were human.

He looked like a king of Earth, not a king of bones. He looked like John David. That startled her at first, but then it made sense, considering the kind of land they were in and what kind of power John David was.

"Can you help?" she asked the Horned King.

"I can," his companion said. Where the light fell, the bones covered over with skin, and Elen saw a woman's face to go with the voice she had heard. It was a striking face, narrow and proud, with eyes as black and sharp as obsidian. "I have no power over living flesh, but listen and do as I say, and mare and foal will live."

Elen glanced at Ria. Her eyes were blank, gone completely empty with terror.

Sara was not quite so far gone, but she was not saying anything, either. Elen was the only one who still had words to say. "I'm not sure if I can—"

"Listen," the woman said, "and do."

She instructed Elen to kneel behind Grace's tail. With the woman's voice in her head, Elen felt her hand guided into the warm wet place. She had to work against the crushing grip of the muscles, and find the foal's neck where it was curved back, and then the blunt contour of the head, and work them around until the neck was straight.

"I'm not strong enough!" she wailed in the dark.

Other hands eased hers out and went in. She looked up into Ria's face. Ria had come to her senses, though she looked as if she had been hit over the head with a hammer.

She was not strong enough, either, and Grace was growing weaker. There was no room for two in there.

Elen had never done what came into her head to try. Maybe it came from Blanca; maybe from the queen of the Hunt. Maybe it was a story she had heard long ago in Ymbria.

"Ria," she said, "I need your magic."

"But I can't—" Ria said.

"You have to," said Elen. "I can tell you what to do. You just need to do it."

"Why can't you? You've got magic, too. Everybody does."

Elen breathed deep and worked hard for patience. "I don't know how to use it. You do. Here. Give me your hands."

Ria clenched her fists. Elen pulled them over toward Grace, toward the mare's flank where the baby was. Ria resisted at first, but then she let out a sound like a sob and gave way.

"Yes," said the lady of the Hunt. Her voice was like a sigh of wind. "Feel the shape inside. Feel the pain. Feel the power that is in you, that pours forth from the land and the air and the sky."

Elen could feel it. It was like Blanca in a way, something outside of her that was still a part of herself. Blanca was in there. So was Moondance, and the other worldrunners. They all were. They were all together.

She laid her hands over Ria's. Their eyes met. Elen saw no hate there. Not even dislike.

She did not feel any, either. That was strange. But there was no time to wonder at it. The foal could not last much longer. Neither could Grace.

"Sara," Elen said. Her voice sounded faint and far away. "Help. Reach inside. Find the head."

Sara dropped to her knees behind Grace. She was the smallest of the three of them, but that meant she could reach where they could not, and turn where they had no room. The magic that flowed through Ria into Elen made her strong.

"Now!" Elen said. All three of them working together turned the head and guided the nose up and out along the curve of the legs.

All at once there was a foal in the wet and bloodied sand, lying in a pool of the sac that had carried it. It lay still for so long that Elen almost cried. It was too late. They had failed. The baby was dead.

Then it lifted its head and rolled onto its front, with its ears all droopy and curly and its lips working, hunting for its mother's milk.

They all broke out in a wild chorus of cheers. Some of the Hunters' voices sounded as if they came from far underground, but they were as purely glad as the rest. Above them all rang Moondance's shrill stallion peal, and the deep whinnies of the mares: Blanca's deepest of all, thrumming in Elen's bones.

Grace sat up, too, to Elen's enormous relief. She was exhausted, but she was alive. Elen's heart, or maybe Blanca's, knew she would be well. Grace curved her head around and flared her nostrils and whickered.

That was the sweetest sound in the world—any world. The Hunt went quiet, and so did Elen and Sara and Ria.

They all moved away so that mother and baby could get to know each other. The queen said, "You'll need to watch all night, make sure the foal stands and nurses and—"

"We know," Sara said gently. "You have all our thanks, from our hearts. But for you, this foal would have died."

"And her mother, too," said Ria. "You've saved both their lives."

"Thank you," Elen said simply. She bowed low, as one should to a queen.

"We who have no life left are more than glad to give what life we can," the woman said. She smiled and bowed and melted into the night.

The others were gone by the time Elen saw the last of her. The king was the only one left.

Elen had been too frantic and then too happy to be afraid. Now she wondered if she should be. "Thank you," she said again. "You kept your promise. We're very, very grateful."

He smiled, and his smile was warm. He looked

more than ever like John David. "You did a brave thing tonight," he said. "It will be remembered."

"Is that bad?" Elen asked.

He laughed, but not really at her. "It was right," he said.

That might have been all, but he paused. His deep eyes lifted to the sky with its crowds of stars. When he lowered them, much of his bright mood was gone. "Stay until morning. Watch over the foal. But when the sun rises, go, and quickly. Delay as little as you may. The sooner you come to Earth, the safer you will be."

Elen opened her mouth to ask what he had seen, but there was no one there. He had vanished with the rest of the Hunt. The night was quiet, empty of either magic or terror—except the living magic in the corral, standing up on long wobbly legs.

CHAPTER 21

It was a filly—a girl. She was coal black, with a tiny star in the middle of her forehead, but there was a sprinkle of white hairs around her eyes. She would be grey when she grew up, like Moondance. He was her father, after all. He made sure everyone knew it.

Long before the sun came up, the filly found the milk she had been looking for. What went in one end came out the other, just as it should.

The watchers could have rested for a little while then, but they were horse girls. They stayed up, drinking in the wonder of each new thing the baby did.

Nobody talked about what the Horned King had said, but Elen could feel it hanging in the chill night air. Elen went into the house, somewhere in the middle, and brought out water and apples and crusty brown bread that had been waiting for her in the kitchen.

"Is that safe to eat?" Ria asked.

"Everything's safe here tonight," Elen answered.

Sara ate without worry. Ria was slower. She had eaten while she was in Caledon, but that had been a long time ago. Eventually she gave in and devoured her share.

No bindings of evil magic tightened around them. Nothing they ate turned to fire in their bellies. It quieted hunger, that was all, and relaxed Elen enough that she dozed a little, propped up against the fence.

The baby bounced in and out of her dream. She had sorted out her legs and got them working together, and was practicing walk and canter and mad gallop all over that corner of the pen. If she tried to investigate the other mares, she faced a wall: her mother with flattened ears and snapping teeth.

She learned quickly, though Elen doubted the lesson would hold for long. While it did, Grace took the opportunity to do what any sensible horse will do after a hard night's work, and eat her way through a manger full of hay.

She was building strength. Even worldrunners were

not strong enough to keep Faerie at bay forever. Time was running out, and so were the safeguards around the canyon.

"Sun's coming," Sara said.

Elen nodded. Ria shivered.

"I'll see if the house has anything left for us to eat," Elen said. "You two start saddling horses. We've got to get on the road before the sun comes up."

The house was dim and quiet. The shadows were very dark. Elen found bread and apples in a cupboard, and a bucket that she filled with water from the pump by the door, to fill their bottles.

Sara had Hera mostly saddled. Elen ran to do the same for Blanca. While she did that, Ria finished grooming Moondance and tried to get his bridle on, but he was having none of it. When she brought the bit up toward his mouth, he spun and darted into the barn.

Ria snarled and ran after him. She was rather a long time coming out. When she did, she wore a be-mused expression, and Moondance wore a handsome saddle.

It was not new. New was stiff and uncomfortable and no good for riding until it was broken in. This saddle was who knew how many years old, but it was in beautiful repair. It fit Moondance perfectly.

He strutted in it, as proud as a prince with a new crown. Even through her worry about the baby and the road and whatever the Horned King had seen on it, Elen had to smile.

Blanca was quiet and very calm. Elen felt the urgency underneath, the sense that they had not much time to waste. She led Blanca to the fence and clambered up the rails into the saddle.

Ria and Sara were busy mounting and rounding up mares. Elen had time to realize how right it felt to be on Blanca. The bay mare she had ridden from Caledon was lovely, and so was Chica back on Earth. But Blanca was home.

Elen looked up. She could see the canyon's rim. A faint line of light marked it.

Blanca was standing perfectly still, but the ground under her moved. It swelled and then sank, as if it breathed.

"We have to go," Elen said.

Her voice was steady. That surprised her.

Sara nodded. Ria's face was stark white. "That shrug in the earth—it's going to break. This place is going to break."

"What—" said Sara.

"Ride," said Ria. Her voice was strung thin with tension. "Just ride."

The mares bunched together around Grace and the baby. Sara set Hera behind them. Moondance sprang into the lead.

Blanca went last. Elen would have been happy with

armor, just then, and as many weapons as she could carry. She did not even have a riding whip. Just Blanca's hooves and teeth, and whatever magic she might dare to use. On the worldroad through Faerie, that would be little or none.

They had to get to the road first. She expected Moondance to start the climb up the canyon walls, but he turned instead and followed the line of the wash. That, she happened to notice, was straight. Perfectly so.

The ground started to shake again. Stones rattled down off the walls. Some of them were big: they bounced and rolled as they came.

There was enough light now to see. Elen knew better than to look back, but she could not help herself. She saw the rock that flattened the barn and crashed into the house.

"The road is safe," Sara said. She must be trying to convince herself. "The road is always safe."

"Is it?" said Ria. "We heard rumors in Caledon: tales of roads broken and things coming through. Nothing is safe any more."

"Because of our war," Elen said.

"It has to end," said Ria.

"That just occurred to you?"

Ria rolled her eyes at Elen. "Oh, please. Don't tell me *you* don't want to keep it going past the end of the universe."

"I don't," said Elen.

Ria did not believe her. But she would. Elen promised herself that. She would show Ria that an Ymbrian, even this Ymbrian, could change her mind.

The horses could go no faster than was safe for the baby. She trotted bravely at her mother's side, but she was so very young still. All too soon she would have to stop and nurse.

They could only do their best. And pray. That might help. It certainly could not hurt.

Elen wrenched her eyes away from the disaster behind. The road aimed straight through the canyon and out into growing daylight. The walls narrowed there, leaving just enough space for the road to run through.

The closer they came, the narrower the space was. The walls were closing—and the light was the wrong color for sunrise. It was red, like fire. It came and went in bursts.

Blanca had speeded up to match pace with Hera. Elen met Sara's wide, fixed stare. Her own must be just the same.

"Firedrakes," Elen said.

Sara nodded.

All they could do was keep going. The baby had

wanted to bounce around at first, but now she clung close to her mother. Her tiny curly ears and her bit of curly mane bobbed in and out of Elen's view.

They were almost to the canyon's mouth. It was closing visibly—slowly but surely. Elen kept her eyes fixed on it, as if her little human will could hold back the power of Faerie.

She could see them in the sky now above the walls, shapes like wide-winged black birds: ravens, maybe, or vultures. But they flew far higher and were far, far larger than any bird. They were dragons of the air, and they breathed fire.

As she watched, one did just that: a tiny spurt of flame. Then the others followed, one after another. It was beautiful, like a procession of candles through the rising dawn.

Moondance had reached the canyon's mouth. It was barely as wide as a man was tall. He paused there; Ria looked back.

"Go on!" Elen wanted to scream at her. "Don't stop! Idiot!" But she kept quiet. After a terribly long instant, Ria faced forward again, and Moondance trotted through the gap. The mares trotted after, with the baby in the middle, scrambling a bit on the sandy footing.

Blanca was the last to go through. The walls of rock were hardly wider than she was. Elen forgot she was not riding an ordinary horse and kicked Blanca as hard as she could.

Blanca ignored her. The walls nearly scraped Elen's knees as she rode through. They ground shut on the very end of Blanca's tail. A piece of it, a handful of white hairs, grew like bleached grass from the solid rock.

They were all out and safe, if safety was hanging in midair, hundreds of feet above any solid ground. The road ran straight through the tarnished silver sky. Elen could see through it, down and down to a jagged and merciless wasteland, a wilderness of stone.

Firedrakes swarmed above and below and all around them. One dropped down upon them—and fell *through* them.

If Elen ever became a ghost, she would never, for the love of the gods, walk through walls. It was the eeriest sensation imaginable. It itched; it was cold, and yet it burned. It made her feel as if she was only half there, and that half was scraped raw.

"Elen!"

Something flashed through the air. Elen caught it without thinking. It was her medallion on its ribbon, with its images of mountain and star.

"You can use this better than I can," Sara said.

"What—" Elen said. "What are you doing?"

"We can't let the road lead us," Sara said. "We have to go back fast, and as straight as we can. This is our guide."

"But I thought the horses were—" Elen bit her tongue. What did she know, after all? She hung the medallion around her neck and closed her fingers over it. The raised lines of the design pressed against fingers and palm.

They felt oddly real, as if they truly were a mountain and the fire of a star. The memory of Earth was in them: the dust of the penning arena, the smell of cattle, the fierce heat of summer even after the sun had gone down.

The road was more solid underfoot. The firedrakes drew back.

Elen dared to breathe—and the road went almost transparent. Flames roared around it. A massive, scaly black body crashed into it behind Blanca, rocking it on whatever moorings held it in the sky.

The firedrake was as hot as iron in a forge, and it had the same fierce metallic smell. Its massive jaws snapped; its claws scrabbled for a foothold. Its leathery wings drove waves of stinking air toward the horses.

Far ahead, Ria's voice came shrilling back. "Run! If you love life, *run*!"

They bolted, even the baby—all but Blanca. She held the rear, braver than any horse should sanely be. Any instant, the firedrake was going to belch flame, and horse and rider would burn.

Elen had no defense but the medallion and her memory of Earth. She raised both between Blanca and the firedrake.

It faded like a mist in the sun—but it did not go

quietly. Its claws flailed as it slipped off and through the road. Each huge curved talon was as long as Blanca.

She stumbled. Elen stared blankly at the deep gouge in her hindquarters. That could not be bone inside. Could it?

Blanca groaned, but she kept moving. The fire-drake roared. The road was closed to it again, and its lungful of flame, bursting forth at last, drifted harmlessly through Blanca and her rider.

Elen slipped out of the saddle. Her heart was breaking. Blanca was hurt. Oh, gods, she was hurt. Elen's eyes burned with tears.

That burning was anger. It made her strong. She forgot exhaustion, and the spike of pain in her back and side just about where the firedrake had torn at Blanca, and the untold miles and gods knew how many worlds they had to fight through before they made it back to Earth. If they made it at all.

"We're going to get there," she said to Blanca. "It will probably kill me, but I'm going to see you all make it back alive. You, too. Especially you."

CHAPTER 22

Once the road was solid and protected, the mares slowed down again. They paused once for the baby to drink thirstily, while firedrakes hovered and circled.

"Can they break through?" Ria asked.

"I don't know," Sara said. "God, I hope not."

Elen barely paid attention. She was trying to do something, anything, to help Blanca. The wound was horrible but it bled little: the heat of the dragon's claw had cauterized where it struck. She thought of covering it with her jacket, but that would only make the pain worse.

All she could do, in the end, was try to make Blanca

drink from the water bottle, and keep herself focused on getting back to Earth. Sara and Ria had nothing more to offer. They both looked sick when they saw what had happened; Sara hugged Elen quickly. "We'll get her home. She'll be all right."

"Yes," Elen said. "Please, yes."

Belief had substance here. Maybe if Elen believed that Blanca could heal, it would happen.

There was no miracle, no magical closing of the wound. Blanca stood with her head down. Her presence inside was faint and dim. She was aware of Elen, but she had no energy to say or think or feel anything except, *Breathe. Keep breathing.* Elen wrapped her arms around the big white neck and tried not to cry.

When the baby finished drinking and they could move on, Sara took the lead. Ria and Moondance came around behind Blanca. The stallion flared his nostrils at the combined smell of mare and injury; he rumbled in his throat, with a hint of a squeal.

If Ria had said anything, Elen would have either snapped her head off or burst into tears. But Ria was wise and kept silent.

Elen was strangely glad to have her there. She had magic that she knew how to use, and the stallion she rode would make sure no harm came to his mare. Elen was past caring if someone else did better at this deadly game than she did—even a Caledonian. She only wanted to get Blanca home.

She ran her hand along Blanca's neck. It was tight, and she was sweating. "Just a little while longer," Elen said to her, not even knowing if it was true. "We'll be there before we know it."

Blanca ducked her head and coughed. Elen could not tell in the weird grey light of this world if what came out of her nostrils was blood.

Elen kept Earth in her head, and most of all the part of Earth called Arizona, with all its jagged edges. She needed that fierceness. She needed those mountains, those spiny cacti, and that relentlessly blue sky.

Ria's hand came to rest on her shoulder. "Almost there," Ria said. She had dismounted and was leading Moondance beside them. Just as it had when the baby was born, her touch fed strength into Elen.

It was not enough to heal Blanca. Maybe nothing was. But it made both Elen and Blanca stronger. It gave them what they needed to keep going.

It was a powerful gift. Ria gave it without hesitation—as any horse girl would. Because Blanca needed it.

Blanca needed Earth. Elen took that need and her own desperation and Ria's strength. She put them all into a single word. "Earth," she said. "We need Earth."

The air rang with the power of that name. The firedrakes shrieked in rage, whirled and spun away. The sky darkened and filled with stars.

Elen had learned their names one night on the

ranch: the Great Bear turning endlessly around the Pole, and Scorpio with Antares like an ember in its heart, and Cygnus the Swan flying through the silver veil of the Milky Way. They were strange names and beautiful, and they belonged surely and only to Earth.

The mares and the stallion and the three riders hung above the earth like the Swan. Their road was moonlight and darkness.

Blanca's walk had slowed. She was breathing hard. That frightened Elen.

"Sara," she said. "Sara, where are we? Where is the ranch?"

Sara hung beside her, bent over Hera's neck. There were lights below, a crowd of them heading up toward the horizon and fading to stragglers below and around her. It looked like a city, and a large one. The road pointed straight down toward it.

Sara's breath rushed out as if she had been holding it. "That's Tucson. Which means the ranch is . . ." She paused, peering into the dark, then pointed. "There."

There was far off into the dark, where black shapes of mountains blocked out the stars. Lightning played along the peaks. Thunder rumbled. It felt as if it had settled in Elen's gut.

"How far?" Elen asked.

"Twenty, thirty miles," Sara said. "Not too far."

Elen had learned what a mile was. Even one, now,

was too far for Blanca. "Can we make the road take us there?"

She was talking to the worldrunners as much as to Sara. None of them answered. Blanca was too far gone. The rest saw no reason to listen to Elen. She was not *their* rider.

Elen cursed them for idiot horses, but they did not care. They were what they were. No human was going to change that.

"You'll have to show us where to go," she said to Blanca. "Please, Blanca. Just try. We've got to get you home."

Blanca barely even heard. Her head was low, and she was wheezing.

"Sara," Elen said. And then, a little less willingly: "Ria. Make your horses listen."

"I'm trying," Sara said. "I can't talk to Hera the way you talk to Blanca. I can't—"

Elen cut across the rest of it. "Ria! Tell Moondance: make the road go to Rancho Estrella."

"Moondance says the road goes where it goes." Ria's frustration was as strong as the scent of thunder. She tried to pull the stallion's head around, but he set his neck against her, threw up his head and jibbed. She slipped and almost went off.

There was nothing else they could do. The road was leading them all. None of them had the strength to take control of it.

They half fell, half slid to Earth in the middle of the strangest place Elen had ever been in. It reminded her of the city of bones, with its rows and rows of empty skeletons. But these bones were metal, and there was no Horned King that she could see.

"The Boneyard," Sara said. The sound that came out of her was half a laugh and half a sob. "That's what they call it. It's the place where airplanes go to die."

Elen knew about airplanes. They had no lives or minds of their own, but there was strong magic in them, magic of metal and plastic and complex machinery.

They loomed all around her, rank after rank of scarred and faded fuselages, battered wings, and tails standing straight up as if there was still hope that they could roar through the sky again. She smelled the sharp smell of desert rain along with the smells of dust and metal and ancient oil, but the storm was long gone, leaving empty creeks and stray puddles.

Somewhere among the metal carcasses, a coyote yipped. An owl swooped overhead. Elen's feet crunched on dried grass and sun-crisped weeds as she moved among the horses. The mares were unhurt; the baby was alive, on its feet, and nursing with loud smacking and slurping sounds.

They were all safe, if tired. Except Blanca. She

stood with her nose almost on the ground. Just looking at her made Elen want to wail at the sky.

The Boneyard had a high, barbed fence around it,
and padlocked gates. None of them was getting over
or through that. Elen stalked up to Moondance and
gripped his bridle and shook him as hard as she could.
"You're the worldrunner! *Get us out of here!*"

Moondance's ears drooped. His head sagged.

It was an answer, if not the one Elen wanted. She
let him go with a guilty pat. Any instant now, she was
going to burst out bawling.

"Did you bring a cell phone?" Ria asked Sara, away
on the other side of Moondance.

"*No*, damn it," Sara answered. "The one and only
time I forget to bring it with me, that's the time I actually need it. I don't suppose you brought one? Or a
magic wand? Or a quarter for a pay phone?"

"That I have," Ria said. She rummaged in her
pockets and pulled out a handful of coins. Some of
them were definitely not minted on Earth, but a good
portion of them were.

Time was when Elen would have said something
cutting about Caledonian thievery. Now she was just
glad Ria had money, though where she would spend it,
Elen could not imagine.

But Sara could. "There's a service plaza down the
road," she said. "We can walk to it; it's not that far."

"I'll go with you," Ria said.

Sara paused as if she ran through objections in her head, but then she nodded. "This late at night, you never know." She raised her voice slightly. "Elen, will you be all right here? Nothing's getting in unless we bring it, but if you want one of us to stay . . ."

"Go," Elen said. She trusted Sara not to abandon them all in this strange and barren place. Ria?

Yes. She trusted Ria. Ria would do anything she possibly could to keep the horses safe.

"We'll be back as fast as we can," Sara said. "You can let the mares drink if there's a puddle—I think I heard they cleaned up anything bad that might have seeped into the ground here. Do watch out for sharp things in the grass. And—"

"I'll be watchful," Elen said. "Go on. Please."

Sara glanced at Blanca and started to say something. Ria pulled her off toward the all too distant fence.

Good for Ria. Elen stayed next to Blanca as they disappeared around the looming shadow of an airplane. The last she heard, they were talking about digging under the fence. Ria had something magical in mind, which Elen could feel in her skin.

They would get out somehow. Help would come. Elen clung to that as she settled to watch over the horses.

The mares were staying close together, but they had

started to graze, nosing around in the weeds and the dry grass. The baby flopped down to sleep almost under Blanca's feet.

Her mother grazed close by. That was remarkable: she should have turned savage and chased Blanca and Elen off. But she knew they would never do anything to hurt her baby.

Worldrunners were horses up to a point. After that, they were something else.

Elen loosened Blanca's girth. After a moment's thought, she unfastened it altogether and carefully took both saddle and bridle off. Equally carefully she stowed them on a bit of girder that thrust up out of the ground. It was not a bad saddle rack, considering. She thought about grooming Blanca with a twist of grass and her jacket, but there was too much pain coming off her. She just needed to be left alone.

Elen swallowed hard. No tears. Not here, not now. She loosened the others' girths, too, but left their saddles on and fastened up the reins to keep them from getting broken while the horses grazed.

There was nothing to do after that but wait. She stood beside Blanca and the baby and turned her face to the stars, filling her eyes with them. It did nothing to heal her heart, but then nothing could, as long as Blanca was hurt.

CHAPTER 23

Blanca had started to sway on her feet. If she went down, there was no way Elen could get her back up again. She was a large horse, and Elen was not a particularly large human.

Elen did what she could. She leaned against Blanca's shoulder and wrapped her arm around the wide white chest. "Hold on," she said. "Just hold on."

Blanca seemed to wake when Elen touched her. She stood a little steadier.

She knew Elen was there. It gave her something to focus on besides pain.

Elen prayed, maybe. She hardly remembered, even while she did it.

Horses were so big and strong, but they broke so easily. A cramp of the stomach that would barely slow down a human could kill a horse. A wound like the one in Blanca's haunch . . .

Elen did not want to think about it. She thought about being strong instead, and staying on her feet. She thought about pushing the pain away and making the wound disappear. She thought about worldroads and magic and how a horse could find her way through Faerie.

All of that was Blanca, but it was only the tiniest fraction of her. Blanca was Elen's heart, and if she died, Elen did not know that she could live.

Big old bony-nosed horse with great big platter feet. Elen willed her to keep standing on those feet. Just for a little longer. Just until someone came to help.

Minutes or an hour or a year later, people came walking down the aisle of metal corpses. Sara and Ria led, and John David walked behind them.

There was a stranger with them, a woman in shirt and trousers so plain and yet so oddly patterned that they must be some kind of uniform. As she came closer,

Elen saw the gleam of metal on the collar, an eagle with wings outspread.

Elen knew a warrior when she saw one. She drew herself up straight. Blanca was still on her feet, and still breathing.

The woman nodded to Elen, a brisk greeting. She did not seem terribly perturbed to find one very tired and disheveled Ymbrian and a herd of horses huddled in the middle of the Boneyard.

John David moved past her toward the baby. His glance caught Elen on the way by. "All present and accounted for?"

"Every one," Elen answered.

John David finished running his hands over the filly. "Alive," he said. "Healthy, as far as I can tell. You've done well."

That warmed Elen's heart a little, but it was not the baby who needed help. Not as long as she had her mother. "Please, sir. Blanca—"

John David was already there. Elen was strangely reluctant to surrender the mare to him, after all her waiting and hoping. But she knew better than to let him see. She stepped back, and found herself between Sara and Ria.

It felt right to be there, if only for a few moments. There were horses to move, and rather a long way still to go, down the aisle to the open gate.

Megan and Bran were waiting there with a pair of horse vans, a large one for the broodmares and the baby and a somewhat smaller one for the riding horses. Ria and Sara and John David and the warrior woman helped Megan load the horses.

Elen held Blanca while Bran examined her as best he could by flashlight and headlights. After a while, during which Elen hardly breathed at all, he looked up. "We'll need the clinic at the ranch," he said, "but I'll do what I can for her here."

He cleaned out the wound carefully, gave Blanca a shot of medicine and a bag of fluids, and helped Elen load her next to Hera. He would not let Elen ride in the trailer, but nothing could stop her from riding in the truck that pulled it.

The trailer door boomed shut. Bran latched and locked it. Elen climbed into the truck.

She had never ridden in such a thing before, though she had seen it and its like rumbling up and down the roads on the ranch. It was surprisingly quiet and comfortable inside—not that she particularly cared, with most of her mind focused on Blanca.

Sara must be riding with Megan and John David, but Ria clambered up beside Elen. Part of Elen, the old part, bristled at her presence, but the rest was glad to have her there. She brought the strength of the tribe with her.

It was a long road back to the ranch. Every bump

and turn ached in Elen's body. She could not imagine what it was doing to Blanca.

She was frantic to get Blanca to the clinic, get the vet, do something, anything, to heal that horrible wound. What would happen after that, what consequences they would all face for what they had done, Elen did not think. Could not think.

When at long last they drove through the gate of Rancho Estrella, it felt as if they had been driving for days, but it was less than an hour by the clock in the truck's dash. The worldrunners' barn blazed with light. There were people everywhere, riders and ranch staff, and the riders' barn stood open wide.

The broodmares and the baby went away to their own barn. Hera and Moondance had clean stalls in this one, with a good grooming and a thorough going-over.

Elen was barely aware of any of that. The stall across from the one that had held the badly burned mare was empty, brightly lit and scoured clean, and the woman who had looked after her was waiting with her machines and her chests of medicines.

Bran called out to her. "Gerda! Over here!"

Gerda came quickly out of the stall, pulling on thin, stretchy glimmering white gloves as she walked. Her expression made Elen wonder how often people and horses came in the way these had. There was plenty of urgency, and she was clearly concerned, but she had an air about her as if she saw this kind of wound and worse every day. "Right," she said. "So. What do we have here?"

"Firedrake claw," Elen said.

Gerda nodded. Her eyes were on the wound, measuring, assessing. "Bring her in," she said.

Elen led Blanca to the veterinary stall. Blanca would let no one else touch her leadrope, and Elen was the last one to object. When Elen attached the crossties to her halter and tried to leave so that Gerda and Bran could work on her, she turned into a whirlwind.

Gerda barely blinked, though she was fast enough to get out of the way of those flying hooves. "Bran," she said calmly, "show her how to scrub in."

That was a retreat to the lab for a great deal of hand- and arm-washing with very strong soap. Bran's expression as he showed Elen how to do it was bemused, as if he were seeing something about her that he had not seen before.

Elen cursed herself for blushing. "What? Have I grown a second head?"

He blinked, and by the gods, he blushed, too. "No! No. I just—we don't see this very often."

"A second head?"

He bit his lip. He was trying not to laugh. "A world-runner who insists on one human. Not that it's unheard of. Her line is prone to it. But—"

"Bran!" Gerda's voice was sharp. It cut off the stream of words. Bran shut his mouth carefully and led Elen back out into the veterinary stall.

Elen held Blanca while Bran and Gerda worked on her. It was too late to stitch the wound, even if its size or location would have allowed it. They killed the pain with drugs, cleaned the huge gash and pared the edges, and fed the mare with still more medicines.

She kept her feet through the whole of it, and never fought or panicked. Her nostrils flared, that was all, and her lower lip clenched tight.

Elen held Blanca's head in her arms, though it weighed almost as much as she did. She breathed with the mare. Her heart beat with Blanca's. Every scrap of strength or courage or stubbornness that she had, she gave to Blanca.

By the time Bran and Megan finished, the sun was coming up. Blanca woke slowly from the fog of drugs and pain. She had a canyon in her haunch and an IV in her neck, but she looked like Blanca again.

Even before Gerda said it, Elen knew it was true: "It's a long road yet, but I think she'll come through."

They let Elen sleep in a cot in the stall next to Blanca's. She slept through the day and the night and into morning again. It was a hard, deep sleep, full of dreams that slipped away before she woke.

When she crawled back into the world, Sara was curled up in a chair by the door with her head on her folded arm, sound asleep. Elen had different clothes on than she had gone to sleep in, and she was much cleaner.

She slipped off the cot and tiptoed past Sara. It was daylight outside, and the barn was deserted. There were a few horses in stalls, but no one Elen knew, except for Blanca. Hera and Moondance were gone—enjoying a well-deserved vacation on pasture, Elen hoped.

Blanca was awake, still with the bandage wrapped around her neck and the IV running clear liquid into it, but she was eating hay. She whuffled when Elen slipped into the stall.

She was all there. All of her was inside Elen, a little shaky around the edges, but almost as strong and bright and sublimely calm as she had ever been. Elen hugged her tight for a long count of breaths, just being there, being with her, being too glad even for tears.

Then she could pull back and see what there was to see. The wound looked a shade less horrible than it had when Elen went to sleep. Inside it was starting to mend. Elen leaned gently against Blanca's shoulder for a while, willing strength and healing into her.

It was wrenchingly hard to leave her, but Elen had a body, too, and it was suddenly insistent. She found the bathroom at the end of the aisle, past Blanca's stall.

When Elen came out, she almost collided with Sara. Sara was not the sort to panic unnecessarily, but she looked a bit wild around the eyes.

"I'm all right," Elen said. "I promise. How much trouble are we in?"

"A lot," Sara said.

Elen's heart stilled. "Are you—"

Sara shrugged. "Not sure yet. We've all been waiting for you to come to."

She sounded as if she did not care, but Elen knew her better than that. She was holding on because she had to.

Elen asked the next question without even stopping to wonder if she should. "Where's Ria? Is she all right?"

"Asleep," Sara answered. "She's been in and out, helping keep watch on Blanca."

"That's good of her," Elen said.

"Well," said Sara, "she feels responsible."

"She should!" Elen said with sudden fierceness. But she brought her temper under control; she said, "She did her best to make up for it. Blanca and the baby wouldn't be alive if it weren't for her. We probably wouldn't have made it back."

"It was both of you," Sara said.

That was uncomfortable to think about. Elen shrugged. Before she could think of anything sensible to say, Bran came walking down the aisle with a pair of riders she did not recognize.

She braced to be hauled off to the nearest dungeon, but they had not come for her. They were there to see Blanca.

Blanca basked in their worship, and the worship of the next two people who came by, and the four after that. Blanca, Elen had long since realized, was more than a worldrunner. She mattered in ways Elen was just beginning to understand.

CHAPTER 24

While Blanca held court in her stall, Sara hauled Elen upstairs. That was riders' territory: a corridor that ran the length of the barn, with doors on either side, and at the end a wide open space with a high peaked ceiling and a wall of windows.

Only one, the largest one in the center, looked out on the desert and mountains of Rancho Estrella. The rest in rows on either side showed the many worlds that lay along the straight tracks. There were too many to take in at once, but one must be Caledon, and one had to be Ymbria.

There was a great deal of fire and darkness among

the worlds. Elen would have gone to look closer, but Sara nudged her away from the windows toward a table that was laid with a hero's breakfast.

"Sit," Sara said. "Eat."

At the sight of so much food, Elen's stomach turned over. "I can't."

"Try," said Sara, relentless.

Sara was not going to let Elen go until she did as she was told. She filled a plate with eggs and beans and fruit and chilaquiles, pushed Elen into a chair and set the plate firmly down in front of her and stood over her until she picked up the fork and stabbed it crossly into the mound of chilaquiles.

The first bite made her gag. The second was not so bad. By the third, she realized she was ravenous. Then she had to keep herself from devouring everything in sight. Sara was not quite as starved, but she downed enough bacon and eggs and juice to keep one of the boys going for a week.

With food came a clearer head, and ability to face the truth. The adventure was over. Now it was time for the reckoning. No matter what they had between them, Blanca was not her horse. Elen had stolen her— with the best intentions in any world, but that made no difference—and nearly got her killed. The smallest price she would pay for it was to never ride Blanca again.

Bran was waiting when Elen and Sara came back down into the barn. This time he had come for Elen.

"Can I say good-bye to Blanca?" she asked. Her throat tried to close up, but she pushed the words through.

Bran nodded. His face was stern, but his eyes understood.

Elen tried not to take too long. Blanca looked better, she thought. She let Elen hug her and rub her favorite places: behind her ears, in the groove of her shoulder, and just behind her withers.

Elen drank in the smell of her. Even with the stink of blood and medicine, it was still *her* smell. Elen would never forget it.

Elen's throat hurt and her eyes stung. She kissed Blanca's big soft nose one last time and turned away.

A covered porch jutted out from the back of the barn, looking down on a terrace of wide stone steps. The last of the steps faded into the path that led to the pastures.

The ramada and the terrace together looked like

an amphitheater. The whole secret half of the ranch spread out below it, framed with mountains. Clouds were piling up over them, promising thunder later.

John David was there with a dozen worldriders. They stood like guards around two groups of guests.

One was all male and nearly all tall and redheaded, except for one dark-haired, blue-eyed boy. And one was both male and female, standing in a circle around a tall, dark woman.

"Mother!" Elen lurched toward her. An arm held her back: Bran, warning her with a glance.

Neither side had seen or heard Elen yet. They were fixed on one another. The riders made a wall between them, and there was a crackle of tension, like lightning about to strike.

The Ymbrians wore armor the color of beetles' wings, gleaming strangely in the light of Earth. The queen's gown was glorious, black chased with gold, with a train that poured down over the stone steps.

The Caledonians were much less splendid. Their armor was chain mail, relentlessly plain and practical, and their leader wore a mantle of deep green wool held at the throat with a silver brooch as broad as a shield boss.

It must all have been hideously hot. None of them would ever admit it, of course, even while the sweat streamed down their faces.

The latest battle in the endless war was already well begun.

"Liar and thief to the very last," the queen said. Her voice dripped scorn. "You broke oath, you broke compact. You did a thing that should doom you and your world forever."

"What, lady?" said the king of Caledon. "You think we had a choice? This war has so broken our world, we have nothing left to lose."

"Nothing? Not the land that is left? Not the people who live on it?"

"Little enough you cared for that when you sent your armies to rake it with fire."

"You had invaded our richest province."

"You had set pirates to raid our caravans."

"Because," the queen cried, "you had been raiding ours until our merchants hardly dared to trade among the worlds."

The king's voice rose to a royal bellow. "Half our world is dust and ash because of you!"

"One of our moons is gone because of *you*!"

John David seemed inclined to let the battle go wherever it wanted to go. But Elen had heard all she could stand to hear. "Stop it! Just *stop*!"

Her voice cracked out like a whip. So did someone else's, in the exact same words and the exact same tone.

Ria had come in with Megan. She was clean and

healthy and fed, and her expression matched Elen's sentiments exactly.

She came down beside Elen and stood with feet braced, glaring at her family. Megan followed but made no move to interfere.

One voice might not have got through, but two together had power to startle even those ancient enemies. The king broke off in mid-bellow; the queen's jaw snapped shut. They turned with eyes blazing.

Elen and Ria blazed back. They did not even have to think about it. They were shoulder to shoulder, and that felt amazingly right.

In the sudden silence, Elen said mildly, "That's enough, I think. If there's going to be any fighting here, it had better be with the two of us."

"It was my fault," Ria said. "I stole the horses. I'll pay whatever I have to pay."

"You did steal them," Elen said, "and that was stupid, though you were just doing what your family told you to do. You did your best to fix it. The baby wouldn't be alive now, or back here at the ranch, if you hadn't been there to help."

"I couldn't let her die," Ria said. "I'm sorry about Blanca. So very sorry."

She looked ready to cry. Elen laid an arm across her shoulders. "Blanca is going to be all right. She's not going to die."

Not that Elen had anyone's assurance about that,

but she knew she was right. Blanca would have an awful scar, and she would need a long time to heal, but she *would* heal.

"I put worldrunners in danger," Ria said. "I cost you and Sara and the horses more than you should ever have had to pay."

"We did what we had to," Sara said.

Elen nodded. That was all there was to it.

"You did it because of us." Ria stood stiff and straight, and her chin was up as she faced John David. "I stole the mares and Moondance. I take responsibility for everything. When you judge, judge me. No one else."

The Caledonians did not like that at all. Ria's brother burst out from among the rest. "No! We forced you. We bound you with oaths and duty. It's our fault. *My* fault. *I'll* pay!"

He looked as if he would have gone on, but two of his cousins clapped hands over his mouth and wrestled him down.

Ria never even glanced at him. She kept her eyes on John David. "I take this on myself," she said. "My world has paid enough. We did a mad and foolish thing, because we were desperate. Let the price be mine to pay."

"No," Elen said. "I stole worldrunners, too. I nearly got Blanca killed. Whatever they do to you, they'll have to do to me."

"And me," Sara said beside her.

Elen half spun. "Sara! You can't—"

"We're all in this together," Sara said.

She was not going to back down. Neither was Ria.

Elen had been avoiding her mother's eyes, but in that moment, she looked straight up into them.

She could not read what she saw there. They were dark and perfectly still. All the quick anger that had been in the queen was gone.

John David listened to it all and said nothing. Compared to the king and the queen from the warring worlds, he was a plain and ordinary man, dressed in jeans and a blue work shirt, with worn cowboy boots and an old straw hat. But he was more than a king. He was like Blanca: he *mattered*.

He drew every eye to him simply by standing there. When he looked up, so did the rest of them.

While the humans waged their war with each other, horses had come out of the barn. Blanca still wore the bandage on her neck, though she had slipped her IV. Hera looked like her old, glossy self.

Moondance pushed past them—risking getting kicked by angry mares, but he was too determined to care. He halted at the edge of the topmost terrace. He took a deep breath: his head came up and his nostrils flared. Then he leaped down, all the way down, face to face with Ria.

Sand and gravel sprayed everywhere. Elen's face

and arms stung. Moondance butted Ria with his head, knocking her to her knees.

Ria made no effort to fight back. Elen caught hold of Moondance's head and pulled it around and said, "No."

He snorted. It was not an angry sound. If anything, Elen would have said he was amused. He shook off her hands, reached down, and ever so delicately pulled Ria up by the collar of her shirt.

When Ria was standing upright, swaying a little, Moondance butted her again, not so hard this time. He was trying to knock her off balance and get her onto his back.

Ria was not playing. She kept her feet stubbornly on the ground.

Moondance was just as stubborn as she was. He went down on his knees, swiveled, and butted himself up under her. By the time she realized what was happening, she was where Moondance wanted her, and Moondance was standing upright, as smug as any horse can be.

John David's eyebrows had gone all the way up. There were dropped jaws and startled expressions all over the amphitheater. But the king's eyes narrowed, and the queen nodded slowly. They knew what they were seeing.

So did anyone who knew worldrunners. They could not be forced.

John David put it in words, slowly, as if he pondered the meaning of it. "If a rider wants to travel the roads and the worldrunner does not, the rider doesn't go. That's always been the way."

"Ria stole the horses," Elen said, as understanding swelled up inside her. "But they let her do it."

Moondance tossed his head and stamped. *Yes*, that meant. *Yes, we let her. We wanted her. She belongs to us.*

He was telling everyone what Elen had known since her first day on the ranch. Ria was horse people. Worldrunner people.

So was Sara. So was Elen. She met Sara's stare past Moondance's nose. Without saying a word, she laid her hand on the stallion's neck and leaned lightly against him, just as Sara was doing on the other side. If anyone wanted to get at Ria or the stallion, he would have to go through one of them.

John David nodded as if they had done exactly what he hoped for, and looked past them to the Caledonians and the Ymbrians. "This is a fair judgment, I think," he said. "Your war is ended. If you choose to think of these two as hostages, then you may. Or you may see them as the promise of genuine peace: not a grudging truce, but a real end to all the fighting."

The Ymbrians ruffled like falcons about to tear into their prey. The Caledonians surged forward, reaching for the weapons that they had not been allowed to carry in this place. The queen and the king stood still, making no move to stop them.

Blanca stepped softly up beside Elen. It seemed impossible that those big hooves should not ring on the stone, but she was as quiet as a cat.

Elen wound her fingers in Blanca's mane. The bandage was stiff and a little rough against her palm. She could feel the warmth of the mare's body through it, and the power and the wisdom that lived in it.

She spoke for that. "Worldrunners will see to it," she said.

She did not say it loudly or especially firmly, but Blanca's strength was in it. It stopped both sides as if they had struck a wall.

She said the rest as it came to her, rising up from the place where Blanca was, deep inside. "You thought mortals and Faerie were laying sentence on you, forcing you to send hostages, threatening you with the closing of the worlds. That was bad, but not bad enough, or Caledon would never have tried what it tried. What would Ymbria have tried next, Mother? How were you going to find a way to keep the war alive?"

The queen had no answer, but in her eyes Elen saw the truth. She would have done something. She would have had to. Her people would have forced her, even if she could have resisted.

Elen spoke to her and to the king and to all of

them. "It's not going to happen. It's over. Worldrunners have had enough. Fight again, raise powers again, turn against each other ever, and they will no longer carry humans to or from Caledon or Ymbria. Share the magic, learn to work together, become a—a herd, that's the word they want. Or tribe, maybe. Learn to be one. Or all the worldroads are closed to you."

"*All* of them," Ria said from Moondance's back, with the same surety. "Completely. Forever. Even the ways we used to take before the worldrunners came are closed; we can't ever use them again. If you try them, you die—or worse. If the worldrunners don't take care of you, the Hunt will. But I don't understand—why I—"

"Don't try to understand," said Elen. "Just accept."

They frowned at each other. They were still not exactly friends, but they were on the same side. Horse people's side.

CHAPTER 25

All the other sides of the war were not going to give it up easily, but without worldroads, it was much harder to have a war at all.

Elen thought her mother might actually be relieved. So might the king of Caledon. His warriors were furious, scowling and snatching at weapons that were not there. He simply looked stern.

So, she noticed, did his son who looked like an Ymbrian. That was interesting, and could be a good thing.

There was one last judgment to face. Elen had

hoped it would happen later, after everyone from off Earth was gone, but John David was not about to make it that easy. "You've done a great thing," he said to the three of them, "and a wonderful thing. All the worlds owe you a debt. But as for what you did to make that happen ..."

Elen moved in before the others could. "Don't punish them," she said. "Especially Sara. They only did what they were forced to do—Ria by her family, and Sara by me. I made her go."

"I know," he said. "They tried to convince me I shouldn't punish you, either. But you know how the worlds work. Actions have consequences."

Elen swallowed, but she kept her head up. "They do, and for me they should. Not the others."

"You all broke the rules," he said. He was not angry. He was stating facts.

That made it worse. Elen opened her mouth to try one last defense, but he cut her off. "You're all grounded: all on Earth and only on Earth until I give you express permission to travel elsewhere. And no more riding worldroads until you've earned it."

Elen was ready for the worst. This was not exactly that. In fact it was not so bad at all.

She seized on what really mattered. "Sara isn't being expelled? She can still be a rider?"

"You all can," John David said, "if you earn it."

Elen took a deep breath. Half was relief. Half was

not. "You said no more worldroads. Didn't you mean worldrunners?"

"I don't think your horse would like that," John David said.

"Blanca isn't my—" Elen said before she saw the glint in his eye. She frowned and changed direction slightly. "I did a terribly wrong thing. I stole her."

"*She* stole *you*," John David said. "Between you, you kept everyone alive and relatively well. Considering how little education you've had and how unprepared you were, you didn't do badly at all."

That was high praise—and he had said it in front of everyone. It made Elen blush.

But better than anything was the way Blanca rubbed her big heavy head against Elen and nearly knocked her down, and then insisted on being taken back to her stall and fed apples and carrots and being worshiped and adored until it was time for Elen to go back to being a camper again.

There was a high council after that, with rulers from all the worlds coming in with escorts of worldriders, and agreements and treaties and a great deal more that Elen would have to understand someday. But not now. Now she was one of the tribe again, a camper on Earth's side of the ranch.

Nobody talked about why she had been gone or what had happened to her, but she could tell they knew. For one thing, she was speaking to Ria—and even the boys restrained themselves from commenting on it. They all pretended it was perfectly normal. And after a while, as they all got used to it, it was.

When she had been back for almost a week, she dallied in the cabin in the morning, getting ready for an early ride and then a long siege of cleaning corrals. Ria and Sara had gone to breakfast already; Elen had been slow to wake up, and was hurrying a little, with her mind already jumping ahead of eggs and biscuits and chilaquiles to Chica and one of the trails through the washes.

When she opened the door, she came face to face with a woman who had her hand raised to knock. She looked like one of the ranch hands in jeans and a work shirt, with her thick black hair braided down her back.

It was a long, blankly astonished moment before Elen recognized her. "Mother! What in the world—"

Cerys smiled, lowered her hand and held out her arms. Elen came into them and held on long and tight.

But she was too full of questions to let the moment last forever. "What are you doing here? How did you get away? Has something happened?"

"I ran away," Cerys said with a touch of wickedness, "and nothing has happened that you didn't have something to do with. I think our war may really be over. Not that it will be easy to convince everyone at home, and there's so much to mend and undo, but still, now that the worldrunners have had their say . . ."

"I'm surprised they never did it before," Elen said.

"Maybe they did," said Cerys, "but no one was able to hear."

Elen had not thought of that. She was not sure it was true, either. Horse girls could always hear.

Then again, when had horse girls ever been asked?

John David was a very wise man.

"We're having breakfast," Elen said, "then we're going riding. Do you want to come?"

Cerys' face lit up, but then it darkened. "I can't stay. We're leaving today, as soon as the last treaty is signed. We've already been away longer than we meant to; gods know what people are thinking—or doing—at home."

Elen had not expected anything else. She tried not to be too horribly disappointed. "You'll have to come back, then," she said, "when camp is over. The parents come, and there's a horse show, and we show off what we've learned."

"I would like that," Cerys said, "though camp won't really end for you. You'll be staying here. After camp ends, school for riders begins. You'll be attending."

"We don't know that yet," Elen said. "We haven't passed. There are still tests, classes—"

"You passed," Cerys said. "Your test was a white

mare and a worldroad, and a war that ended because of you."

Elen was having trouble breathing. "But—John David didn't—"

"I'm sure he'll tell you when he's ready," said Cerys. "You can pretend to be surprised. Your friends are staying, too: the girl Sara. And your cousin from Caledon."

She managed to say that name without the catch of old hate. Elen was proud of her. "So we're all staying, all three. We're all in it together." She paused. "It's part of the plan, isn't it? To make absolutely sure the war doesn't start again. I'm in exile. I can't go home."

"You will," said Cerys. "You'll be a rider, and travel to all the worlds. You'll come back to us with honor and lasting glory."

She was sure of it. Elen could only hope she passed all the tests and learned all the lessons and did not make a fool of herself and her whole world.

Cerys hugged her tightly and kissed her forehead. "Just be Elen," she said. "The rest will take care of itself."

Elen had too much pride to burst into tears, but her sight went blurry. Her mother kissed her again and left her, slipping away through the gate in the wall.

CHAPTER 26

Elen and Ria and Sara sat on the back porch of the lodge one evening, a little over two weeks after the worldrunners ended the long war. A monsoon storm had roared and rampaged through in the afternoon, dumping rivers of rain. A burst of wind had ripped the roof off the Clydes' pen, crumpled it like tinfoil, and tossed it a hundred feet into the middle of the roping arena.

Now the world was still and damp and cool, and the lightning had marched off into the mountains. Elen sprawled on the porch swing, rocking it back and forth with a lazy foot. Her jeans were not stiff and new any more; they had started to fade and wear the way jeans should.

"This would be a fine night to ride the worldroads," Ria said.

They all sighed. Elen saw Blanca every day—Blanca insisted on it. But riding her was out of the question, even if she had not been on pasture rest until her wound healed. The next time Elen sat on that wide white back, she would have earned the right through time and work and long study.

Elen was starting to understand how truly mad she had been to do what she did. She had muddled through on luck and ignorance and Blanca's power in the realms of Faerie. If she ever did anything like it again, she would be a full rider and she would know exactly what she was doing.

"Do you think we'll really make it through and become riders?" she asked while the lightning played across the mountaintops.

"Do you want to be?" Ria wanted to know.

Elen's first, unthinking answer was, "Yes." Then after she caught herself, and listened to what she had just said, and took the time to think about it, she said it again. "Yes, I do. Do you?"

"There's never been a rider from Caledon," Ria said. "When we're children, we dream of being the first. Not that I ever seriously expected it to happen. I didn't think it was possible."

"We're not the ones who choose," Sara said. "The ranch isn't, either, though Uncle John has something to say about it. The horses decide. If we're meant for it, we want it. It's like a spell."

"Horses always do that to their people," Elen said.

"It's still our free will," said Sara. She left her chair to perch on the rail, riding it like a horse: walk to trot to canter. She stopped before she rolled off. "I want to be a rider. If I can. If I'm strong and smart and wise enough."

Elen knew what she meant. She felt it inside her. Even through the fear, the not wanting to change, and the constant undertone of homesickness for her own world, she wanted at least to try. To see if she could do it for real and not just because there was no one else who would.

The medallion still lived in her pocket, though she had hardly looked at it since she came off the world-road. It dug into her hip when she shifted her weight on the swing. She pulled it out and turned it in the last of the light.

There they were, just as they had guided her through fire and darkness: the mountain and the star. They were not home, exactly. Not yet. But they were where she needed to be.

Being a rider felt right—someday. They all had a fair bit of growing up to do first.

Nan called from inside the lodge. "Movie Night! Come on in!"

It was racehorse movies tonight, "Seabiscuit" and "Dreamer" and something about a zebra. Elen was not sure she believed in zebras. Horses? With stripes? Ridiculous. The others were determined to prove to her that the creatures were real.

None of them was quite ready to go in yet. They made the evening last for a little while longer, while the dusk deepened and the lightning flashed. Nobody said anything, but they had all seen the glimmering track of the worldroad, rising straight up toward the mountains.

Someday they would ride that road again. That was a promise. Elen felt it deep inside where Blanca was, always, no matter how far apart their bodies were.

"Someday," she said aloud. Then she turned and followed the others into light and air conditioning and the rowdy welcome of the tribe.

ABOUT THE AUTHOR

Caitlin Brennan was born and grew up in Maine. She first sat on a horse, assisted by her grandfather, at six months old. The horse's name was Willie. When her brother William was born, two years later, she refused to believe that he was not named after the horse.

She "officially" rode a horse for the first time at age seven. She has been riding ever since. The first horse she owned was a Quarter Horse who loved to stand on her hindlegs and walk across the road with a rider on her back. This marked Caitlin for life, and resulted in her, eventually, owning Lipizzans, who are equally fond of going airborne at random moments.

Caitlin has lived in New England and in the original England. After she finished school (she has a Ph.D. from Yale), she moved to Arizona and immediately bought her first Lipizzan, a beautiful grey mare named Capria. Capria still lives with Caitlin at Dancing Horse Farm, along with half a dozen other Lipizzan mares and a stallion who is the model for Moondance in *House of the Star*. The stallion's registered name is Pluto Carrma III, but everyone calls him Pooka. Pooka's favorite mare is Pandora, who is the model for Blanca in the book.

Caitlin is a recovering Dressage Perfectionist. She blogs that experience (with pictures) here: http://www.deserthorseinc.com/journal_intro.html.